The Curse of Rocamadour

Louise Dale

Dragonheart
Publishing

Published in Great Britain in 2002
Dragonheart Publishing, The Grey House, Main Street,
Carlton-on-Trent, Newark, Notts., NG23 6NW.

www.dragonheartpublishing.co.uk

British Library Cataloguing in Publication Data.
A catalogue record of this book is available from the British
Library.

ISBN 0 9543773 0 3

Illustration by Ian R. Ward, Mansfield, Nottinghamshire.

The Time Trigger Series:
The Curse of Rocamadour

Typesetting and production by Richard Joseph Publishers Ltd
Printed and bound by Advance Book Printing, Northmoor,
Oxford OX29 5UH. E-mail: advancebp@aol.com

For Emily and Lizzie

Contents

"I found it after the floods, when the river water went down, actually," snapped Alice. "I think it could have been disturbed after hundreds of years."

"Yeah. Whatever". Sarah was once again caught up in the frustrations of her *Game Boy* game.

Alice thought about the worst floods in Newark for hundreds of years. Her house normally stood quite a way from the River Trent, but this year the river had burst its banks. Luckily for Alice's family, the river water only flooded part of their garden. Alice had heard that the experts were still worried about the reasons for the freak conditions. Nothing quite as bad had ever been recorded in Newark, although Alice had read about some unexplained natural phenomenae involving waters and whirlpools in the chronicles of Newark Castle at the time of King John. Now, the experts apparently saw signs of a recurrence in the unusual weather conditions and the local council was on alert again.

Alice yawned. It was too early in the morning for her. She liked her lie-ins. As the coach sped towards London and the English Channel beyond, she let her eyes close and she slipped into a delicious dream about Ice Age mammoth hunts and chanting sorcerers. She rubbed her stone and fought off a desire to suck her thumb.

2

Sunflowers and Goats Cheese

The scenery had changed. As the coach left the French motorway, Alice was greeted by the familiar sight of sunflower fields. The flowers turned their giant nodding heads towards the hot sun. Row upon row of them blended into a magnificent floral carpet. The clear summer sky crashed into the yellow horizon and reflected a turquoise brilliance in villa swimming pools.

Alice could almost smell the fresh peaches and strawberries in the markets and she fancied she could hear the endless zing, zing, zing of the grasshoppers. She sighed contentedly.

"I just saw some grapes! Look, over there on those little bushes."

Robert was leaning round, over the back of his seat, pointing excitedly.

"Vines," corrected Alice.

"Wow! We could pinch a few and squash them to make wine." Robert grinned mischievously.

"I think there's a bit more to making wine than squashing grapes," said Sarah, who was knowledgeable about most things. "Don't you have to mix them with yeast or something?"

Alice stole a glance at Robert. He looked a little deflated, probably because Sarah had ruined thoughts of stamping down some stealthily acquired grapes and getting drunk. Robert's thick blond hair, untidied by the long journey, reminded Alice of a haystack, but she quite liked its messiness.

The coach rounded a sharp corner and started to edge

down a narrow lane with a sign saying *La Grange aux Fleurs*. Miss Walton addressed the occupants of the bus.

"Here we are then. Time to get off!"

The hot air took the young people by surprise after the air conditioning in the coach. It scorched their throats.

"It's boiling!" gasped Robert.

"Good for sun-tans!" said Tessa.

Alice looked down at the fair skin on her arms. Miserably she knew she'd gain loads more freckles, no matter how much sun cream she used.

As they wandered towards the buildings there were cries of approval when they noticed the large swimming pool.

"Looks good!" said Sarah. "I wonder if you can dive into it?"

Miss Walton and Mr Hutchinson were greeted by a rotund Frenchman. He was very brown and spoke in deep French tones. While the adults sorted out the arrangements, Alice and Sarah looked around.

On one side of the pool, across the gravel drive, were two huge converted barns. Their big wooden doors were wide open, and the girls could see benches and tables inside the nearest one.

"Looks like the dining room," suggested Alice, realising she was quite hungry, and wondering how long it would be until someone fed her.

"I can see beds in the other one," said Sarah.

Robert and his friend Luke were already peering through one of the windows in the second barn.

Inside, it had been cleverly adapted into small rooms, each with two sets of bunk beds and a blue lamp on a little bedside table. A sausage shaped pillow lay on top of a neatly folded duvet at the foot of each bed.

Alice noted the pillows with disappointment. She could never get really comfy on those things.

Luke spotted a small pond around the corner of the first barn.

"Hey, Rob! Tadpoles. Hundreds of them!"

"Hope Miss Walton will let us collect some," said Robert. "Oh, look! Some of them have already got back legs."

Alice and Sarah joined them. They all agreed they'd try and get a few tadpoles into a bucket or something, and see what happened to them. While the others were trying to think what they could use to put them in, Alice looked up. Above them, on the edge of the gently sloping field, a dark-haired French boy was watching them. He looked slightly older. He was sweaty and dirty, wearing a very scruffy T-shirt that might have once been green or grey, and denim shorts. Alice couldn't see his feet in the piles of freshly cut hay that lay in ridges up and down the field. He smiled cautiously at Alice.

"Bonsoir."

Alice thought he didn't look all that pleased to see them. She nodded a greeting and said *bonsoir* back. A woman's voice shouted from somewhere over the brow of the hill, followed by a tractor engine starting up. The young man shouldered his pitchfork, turned away and strode athletically up the hill.

Alice suddenly felt dizzy, which was unusual for her. She almost thought she heard a woman sobbing. She closed her eyes, but that made the giddiness worse. Just for a moment she imagined she could see a lady in a long dress, crying in a dark room somewhere. Once again, Alice sensed danger. Then she heard Mr Hutchinson shouting. She flicked her eyes open and shook her head.

"Take your own bags from the pile and put them in your room! There's a list of who's where on that barn door over there."

Relieved that the peculiar feeling was subsiding, Alice followed the others towards the heap of cases on

14

1

The School Trip

Alice Hemstock dumped her suitcase on the school driveway and waved goodbye to her mother. Almost everyone was there. Robert Davenport kicked his bag closer to the rest and smiled at Alice.

"Yes, I know, Mr Davenport. Don't worry." Miss Walton, the French teacher, was trying to sort out some problem with Robert's father. "As long as we've got your mobile phone number, we'll be able to contact you from France if necessary... not that we anticipate needing to, of course... just in case of emergencies!"

Miss Walton looked very anxious. Her thin frame tottered back and forth, and her long nose twitched continuously under a nervous frown.

"Stress!" said Alice to herself with a chuckle.

"Alice!" She turned to greet her friend Sarah. "Come on! If we're first on we'll have a chance at getting the back seat for a change."

Alice swung her rucksack onto her back and followed her friend round to the front of the coach. Unfortunately, Tessa and her little gang were already in place right by the door. Tessa smirked.

Their form teacher Mr Hutchinson walked towards them waving his clipboard in the air.

"Who's the fittest one here?" he shouted.

All eyes turned on Tessa who tried to look modest, but only succeeded in looking smug.

"Tessa? O.K. Good. Run back inside and get the stack of files that's on top of my desk would you? And take your two friends with you to help."

Alice watched with interest as the conceited look on

Tessa's face rapidly faded into silent anger.

"Now, Tessa, please," said Mr Hutchinson.

The three girls sloped into the school building. Unfortunately for them, the driver had just finished loading the luggage. He pressed a button and the coach door hissed open.

"On you get," snapped Miss Walton.

Tessa burst back out through the school doorway clutching some files, just too late to get in front of Alice and Sarah, who deftly slipped onto the coach, down the aisle and into the back seat. They smacked each other's hand in triumph.

After a bit of jostling, and a few menacing glares in Alice's direction from Tessa and her mates, everyone clambered on and sat down. Mr Hutchinson tried to keep his balance on the stairwell at the front as he finished taking the register and outside a few groups of parents stood around waiting to wave the bus off.

Mr Hutchinson cleared his throat. "O.K. Let's set a few ground rules before we start, shall we?"

Alice tried to stuff her over-full bag under the seat in front of her. The C.D. player was sticking out awkwardly and she bent forward to try and straighten it, conscious of the fact that she must be making Robert Davenport's seat feel rather lumpy. All the shuffling and pushing was too much for him.

"Hey!" he whispered back at Alice, through the gap between the seats. "Can't you keep still?"

"Oops. Sorry. Nearly done it." She gave one last shove.

"...and THAT applies to everyone. At twelve years of age we would expect you to be..." Mr Hutchinson stopped talking and frowned. "Alice Hemstock and Robert Davenport, what are you doing?"

Everyone turned to look at them and Robert's face went an unhealthy shade of raspberry pink. Alice wished the floor of the coach would open and swallow her. Tessa started whispering to her neighbours, just loud enough for Alice, and most of the bus, to hear an emphasis on the words "...fancies him."

"Er, sorry, Mr Hutchinson. My bag got stuck," said Alice, trying to look bolder than she was feeling. "I've done it now."

"Oh, good. I am very pleased to hear that," said the form teacher sarcastically. He turned to the driver. "Let's get going then, or we'll miss the ferry if the traffic around London is as bad as usual."

The coach swung round and lumbered off down the school drive and Alice sat back in the corner taking her last glimpses of Newark. As the coach headed over the river towards the motorway, she stared at the crumbling 12th century gatehouse and tower of Newark Castle.

Alice loved history. She was definitely going to be an archeologist. She felt in her fleece pocket for her lucky stone and pulled it out, turning it in the palm of her hand. It felt smooth and cold. A bright light outside momentarily diverted her attention.

The early morning sun was reflected in the castle's empty arches and windows and in the river that flowed beside it. The whole structure looked as if it was on fire. It was wild and magical.

In a flash of imagination, Alice saw a bustling, medieval castle with horses whinnying and men shouting.

"Look, Sarah!"

But as Sarah looked up from her *Game Boy*, the coach turned a corner and the mystical redness vanished instantly.

"What?"

"Oh! It's gone."

"What has?"

"Never mind. The sun was reflected in the castle windows, that's all," said Alice, feeling a little embarrassed.

She sensed something else too, a glint of danger that made her feel uneasy.

"It's not possible for the sun to be reflected in those windows," said Sarah dogmatically, as she returned to her game.

"Why not?"

"Because there's no glass in the windows of this side of Newark castle, silly!"

"Oh, no. But I . . ."

Alice turned back and craned her neck. The mirage was nowhere to be seen. The arched frames of the ancient windows displayed only the black and shadowy interiors of the majestic structure. Alice was puzzled. She felt a shiver run down her spine.

"I did see it, honestly," she muttered under her breath.

"What's that?" asked Sarah, pointing to the polished pebble in Alice's hand.

"It's my lucky stone."

"Can I see?"

"Yeah, but don't drop it. I think it might be valuable."

"Where did you get it, then?" asked Sarah. "Is this one of your crazy stories about ancient treasures or spiral galaxies or something?"

Alice hesitated. She wished she could boast that she had found it in a glamourous grotto that was full of beautiful crystalline stalactites or in an Ice Age city of cave dwellers that reeked with prehistoric mystery, like the ones she'd visited when she stayed with her cousins in France. But Alice was essentially an honest girl, so she opted for the truth.

"In my garden", she said, a little sheepishly.

"Oh, right. A valuable gem, possibly Roman, or even extraterrestrial, from the famous archeological dig in the Hemstock back garden at Newark-on-Trent." Sarah grinned at her friend as she passed back the stone with mock delicacy.

"I found it after the floods, when the river water went down, actually," snapped Alice. "I think it could have been disturbed after hundreds of years."

"Yeah. Whatever". Sarah was once again caught up in the frustrations of her *Game Boy* game.

Alice thought about the worst floods in Newark for hundreds of years. Her house normally stood quite a way from the River Trent, but this year the river had burst its banks. Luckily for Alice's family, the river water only flooded part of their garden. Alice had heard that the experts were still worried about the reasons for the freak conditions. Nothing quite as bad had ever been recorded in Newark, although Alice had read about some unexplained natural phenomenae involving waters and whirlpools in the chronicles of Newark Castle at the time of King John. Now, the experts apparently saw signs of a recurrence in the unusual weather conditions and the local council was on alert again.

Alice yawned. It was too early in the morning for her. She liked her lie-ins. As the coach sped towards London and the English Channel beyond, she let her eyes close and she slipped into a delicious dream about Ice Age mammoth hunts and chanting sorcerers. She rubbed her stone and fought off a desire to suck her thumb.

2

Sunflowers and Goats Cheese

The scenery had changed. As the coach left the French motorway, Alice was greeted by the familiar sight of sunflower fields. The flowers turned their giant nodding heads towards the hot sun. Row upon row of them blended into a magnificent floral carpet. The clear summer sky crashed into the yellow horizon and reflected a turquoise brilliance in villa swimming pools.

Alice could almost smell the fresh peaches and strawberries in the markets and she fancied she could hear the endless zing, zing, zing of the grasshoppers. She sighed contentedly.

"I just saw some grapes! Look, over there on those little bushes."

Robert was leaning round, over the back of his seat, pointing excitedly.

"Vines," corrected Alice.

"Wow! We could pinch a few and squash them to make wine." Robert grinned mischievously.

"I think there's a bit more to making wine than squashing grapes," said Sarah, who was knowledgeable about most things. "Don't you have to mix them with yeast or something?"

Alice stole a glance at Robert. He looked a little deflated, probably because Sarah had ruined thoughts of stamping down some stealthily acquired grapes and getting drunk. Robert's thick blond hair, untidied by the long journey, reminded Alice of a haystack, but she quite liked its messiness.

The coach rounded a sharp corner and started to edge

down a narrow lane with a sign saying *La Grange aux Fleurs*. Miss Walton addressed the occupants of the bus.

"Here we are then. Time to get off!"

The hot air took the young people by surprise after the air conditioning in the coach. It scorched their throats.

"It's boiling!" gasped Robert.

"Good for sun-tans!" said Tessa.

Alice looked down at the fair skin on her arms. Miserably she knew she'd gain loads more freckles, no matter how much sun cream she used.

As they wandered towards the buildings there were cries of approval when they noticed the large swimming pool.

"Looks good!" said Sarah. "I wonder if you can dive into it?"

Miss Walton and Mr Hutchinson were greeted by a rotund Frenchman. He was very brown and spoke in deep French tones. While the adults sorted out the arrangements, Alice and Sarah looked around.

On one side of the pool, across the gravel drive, were two huge converted barns. Their big wooden doors were wide open, and the girls could see benches and tables inside the nearest one.

"Looks like the dining room," suggested Alice, realising she was quite hungry, and wondering how long it would be until someone fed her.

"I can see beds in the other one," said Sarah.

Robert and his friend Luke were already peering through one of the windows in the second barn.

Inside, it had been cleverly adapted into small rooms, each with two sets of bunk beds and a blue lamp on a little bedside table. A sausage shaped pillow lay on top of a neatly folded duvet at the foot of each bed.

Alice noted the pillows with disappointment. She could never get really comfy on those things.

Luke spotted a small pond around the corner of the first barn.

"Hey, Rob! Tadpoles. Hundreds of them!"

"Hope Miss Walton will let us collect some," said Robert. "Oh, look! Some of them have already got back legs."

Alice and Sarah joined them. They all agreed they'd try and get a few tadpoles into a bucket or something, and see what happened to them. While the others were trying to think what they could use to put them in, Alice looked up. Above them, on the edge of the gently sloping field, a dark-haired French boy was watching them. He looked slightly older. He was sweaty and dirty, wearing a very scruffy T-shirt that might have once been green or grey, and denim shorts. Alice couldn't see his feet in the piles of freshly cut hay that lay in ridges up and down the field. He smiled cautiously at Alice.

"Bonsoir."

Alice thought he didn't look all that pleased to see them. She nodded a greeting and said *bonsoir* back. A woman's voice shouted from somewhere over the brow of the hill, followed by a tractor engine starting up. The young man shouldered his pitchfork, turned away and strode athletically up the hill.

Alice suddenly felt dizzy, which was unusual for her. She almost thought she heard a woman sobbing. She closed her eyes, but that made the giddiness worse. Just for a moment she imagined she could see a lady in a long dress, crying in a dark room somewhere. Once again, Alice sensed danger. Then she heard Mr Hutchinson shouting. She flicked her eyes open and shook her head.

"Take your own bags from the pile and put them in your room! There's a list of who's where on that barn door over there."

Relieved that the peculiar feeling was subsiding, Alice followed the others towards the heap of cases on the drive. She glanced behind, but the French boy had disappeared from view.

"Er... just a minute. I haven't finished yet." Mr Hutchinson put on his really teacherly voice. "When you've done that, Madame Magret will be serving supper in the dining room, so WASH YOUR HANDS!"

"He thinks we're flippin' babies," moaned Robert.

"Wonder what we'll get for tea, then?" Robert's friend Luke voiced what several of them were thinking. "No frogs legs I hope!"

Alice, now recovered, gave him a 'you're-so-thick' look.

After everyone made a lot of mess during the enforced hand washing, they drifted into the dining room barn expectantly.

The long wooden tables were simply laid with plastic mats and a knife and fork in each place. There were large bowls of salads, tomatoes and strawberries and painted plates crammed with French meats and goat's cheese. Jugs of apple and orange juice stood here and there and something that Alice suspected was iced tea. She would avoid that.

"Yes!" she exclaimed, when she saw the huge baskets of French bread.

She slept soundly that night.

The next morning Alice climbed down from her top bunk and peeped through the curtains. Sure enough, the sky was still a deep turquoise blue and there wasn't a cloud in sight. She glanced at her roommates, but they were still and quiet. She silently slid on her jeans, tucked in the T-shirt she'd slept in and grabbed her trainers. Thankfully, the door handle turned smoothly and she escaped into the morning freshness. After a quick inspection of the pond while she smoothed her strawberry blond hair into a scrunchy, she strolled down the gravel driveway bathed in the warm sun.

Some yellow limestone rocks in the ditch caught her

attention. She bent over and gently parted the long grasses to get a better look. There was a sudden movement and Alice jumped back as a thin black snake darted across the top of the nearest boulder. She stumbled backwards and was surprised to see the dark-haired French boy a few paces behind her.

The boy shot a glance at the rocks and seemed to understand what must have happened.

"Ça va?" he asked.

"Oui. Ça va," Alice replied automatically. *"Un... un..."*

The French word for snake momentarily eluded Alice.

"Un serpent?" suggested the boy.

"Oui," nodded Alice.

They continued to converse in French.

"You speak French?" the boy asked her in some surprise. "That is not usual for you English kids."

Alice thought he seemed quite impressed.

"Some of my family live in France," she said. "My aunt and cousins. Not far from here in fact. At Montignac. I stay with them quite often."

"Ahh". Alice knew he was impressed now.

Alice found herself slipping easily into French conversation. Even her mannerisms became subtly different. Her voice became more musical and she relaxed into near perfect pronunciation, only faltering when she didn't know the French word for something. The young Frenchman found it very funny when she told him that she liked last night's legs instead of last night's ham for supper.

"I think you mean *jambon*, not j*ambes*!" he said, momentarily speaking in English. He grinned kindly at her.

They sat down on the low wall that ran along the drive. The stone in Alice's jeans pocket jabbed her leg, so she took it out and started rubbing it, as was her habit.

16

"What is that? May I see?" asked the French boy enthusiastically.

Alice was pleased with his interest.

"Sure. Unusual isn't it?" She passed it over.

He scrutinized the worn pebble intently, turning it over and over between his fingers.

"Where did you get it?" he asked eventually, in his rich, French voice. His dark eyes were alert with curiosity.

"It was washed up in my garden by a flooded river."

"In England?"

"Yes, of course."

He seemed disappointed.

"Why?" asked Alice. For some reason she began to feel a shivery sensation. She took the stone back from the boy's palm. It felt icy cold, which was odd, as he had been handling it and Alice expected it to feel warmer.

"Oh, it's nothing, really."

The French boy stood up.

"But you were so interested. Please, tell me why."

"It's nothing. Really it isn't. It's just ... very similar to something I have seen before."

Alice stood up next to him.

"What thing that you have seen? Where?"

The French boy hesitated. He seemed uncertain whether or not to trust her. Alice was aware that he was appraising her and she wondered if he liked her. She must be quite different from most of the girls he knew, who would have nut-brown skin at this time of year.

"I like your accent," he said at last. "It's funny."

There was a slightly awkward pause. Then he spoke with sudden impulsiveness.

"I have a stone that is very similar."

Alice looked at him in astonishment.

"Where did you get yours?"

"I found it stuck in one of the ancient walls of our

farmhouse. People say there was a castle here hundreds of years ago and what was left of it was built into our house."

Alice raised her eyebrows. "Wow!"

"I always thought my stone had been broken in half," he said. "It has a sharp edge on one side."

"Could I ...", Alice hesitated.

"What?"

"Could I... see it sometime?"

At that moment, someone banged a gong down in the courtyard.

"I suppose so. I could meet you after breakfast. Will you be able to get away?"

"I'm sure I will!" Alice knew she would find a way. "Where?"

"Come to the gate of the farmhouse... just over there. I'll meet you."

"O.K." replied Alice, trying not to look too keen. "Oh. By the way, what's your name?"

"Jean-Marc. Jean-Marc Magret. And yours?"

"My name's Alice."

"See you later Alice from England!"

3

A Feeling of Magic

Breakfast looked wonderful. The long tables were littered with baskets of fresh *baguettes* and *croissants* and steaming jugs of milky coffee.

Alice squeezed in next to Sarah.

"Where were you?" whispered Sarah.

"I went for a walk," said Alice in a matter-of-fact sort of voice as she poured coffee into a bowl and began dipping her bread into it, in the way she always did when she was in France at her aunt's house.

"Yuk! That looks horrible!"

"Actually, it's great. You should try it," encouraged Alice, relieved that she had distracted her friend. She was thinking rapidly, trying to work out how to slip away to meet Jean-Marc.

"What are we doing today?" she asked.

"We're going to some town built into the rocks I think," said Robert from the other side of the table. "It's got eagles and vultures and buzzards and things!"

"Yeah, but will we get to see them do you think?" groaned his friend Luke. "Mr Hutchinson said we had to do a project on pilgrims or something boring like that!"

"And I wanted to go swimming," said Sarah, grumpily.

"Yes, we ARE going to visit the eagle sanctuary," came a stern voice from behind. "After that, we're having a tour of the chapels and crypts."

Unfortunately, Miss Walton was standing there, pouting her thin lips disapprovingly.

"And you WILL be able to use the swimming pool when we get back," she added deliberately. She marched off towards the front of the barn and cleared her throat.

"As some people seem to have forgotten their schedules, I will run through the programme for today." She cast a disapproving glance in the direction of Alice's table, which brought sniggers from Tessa and her gang. "The coach leaves at ten. It's a busy timetable. We're going to the spectacular city of Rocamadour that has been built into the cliffs of a canyon. We have booked a tour of the 12th century Chapel for two o'clock this afternoon. If there's time, we'll have a little look around the town itself. Mr Hutchinson and I thought you might like to visit the *Rocher des Aigles*, or eagles' rock, which is a sanctuary for birds of prey, before lunch if there's time."

There was a general murmur of approval.

"So I'd like you all to take your plates over there and put them into those plastic bowls for washing up. Then you may clean your teeth, etcetera." She looked at the watch on her bony arm. "Be by the coach with your project files at a quarter to ten. Do you want to add anything, Mr Hutchinson?"

Their form teacher stood up. Mr Hutchinson looked as if the heat was making his stout body and balding head perspire uncomfortably.

"Er, hum ... I want you to remember that you are representing your school. Please behave properly at all times. No pushing or shouting. Off you go."

They all scrambled to dispose of their dirty crockery and drifted towards the dormitories. Alice hung back. She bent down, pretending to adjust her trainer and peered cautiously about. Everyone seemed distracted and she casually took a few paces to the edge of the barn and ducked round to the back. From there it was easy to reach the upper branch of the farm drive where it forked towards the sloping hay fields that spread up the hill. She doubled back on herself and ran down towards the farmhouse nestling in the hillside below the barns of *La*

Grange aux Fleurs. As she rounded the bend in the drive she saw Jean-Marc in front of her, dragging gravel into swirling patterns with his foot. He looked up and smiled.

"Did you have any problems getting away?"

"Not really. I've got about half an hour before the coach leaves."

He beckoned to her to follow him and they turned into the private drive towards his home.

"What a lovely house!"

Alice could tell it was very old. The plaster was cracked and crumbly in places. The tall windows were flanked on either side by worn, blue shutters and lace curtains were stretched prettily on the inside of the glass. Stone steps led up to the door and there was a terra-cotta flowerpot on each one. Bright red trailing geraniums cascaded from the pots. A gnarled vine wound its way up the wall beside the front door and over the top across a slatted wooden porch. Alice could see the tiny, unripe grapes tumbling down between the slats like bunches of green marbles.

The gravel drive widened into a courtyard in front of the house, then continued past into a stony walnut grove. Neat rows of well-kept vines stretched endlessly away from the house down the gentle slope of the hill-side.

There was nobody about and she followed Jean-Marc into an open-fronted barn on one side of the house. He climbed a wooden ladder to the loft above. Alice hesitated.

"It's O.K. It's quite safe."

Jean-Marc held out his hand and Alice cautiously followed him. He helped her onto the dirty platform and as Alice's eyes adjusted to the dim light, she began to make out the furnishings of the den. There was a tatty arm-chair with tapestry cushions and books and piles of comics strewn over a worn rug. Alice's eyes widened as she saw the cluttered shelves of an old bookcase, which were filled with an exotic collection of what looked like fossils, rocks and minerals, and a variety of sharks' teeth. There were jars of pebbles and coloured sands and a dusty microscope.

"Wicked!" murmured Alice.

Jean-Marc took a metal box from the top shelf and fiddled with the clasp.

Alice suddenly drew her breath.

"Oh, no! Not again..." She had started to feel very giddy. She blinked and steadied herself on the back of the armchair, closing her eyes. Her breathing quickened. Once again, she saw a vision of long ago but this time, it was much clearer.

Behind a studded castle door, a young man paced back and forth across a dingy room. Alice thought he looked like some kind of prince. Outside an eagle circled close to the castle tower and its cries echoed round and round the vaulted chambers. Standing in the light of flickering oil lamps was a young woman with long black hair. She grasped a stone pendant that hung around her graceful neck. She sighed deeply and began to speak. Incredibly, Alice realised she could hear her.

"Oh, John! I can never marry you while Richard lives. I have told you so many times. All those years that we were growing up together in England, it was as Richard's intended wife, not yours. I know he does not love me. But it is my duty. If I defy him he may take some terrible revenge on my people and on you..."

"Bah! I'm not afraid of my brother! Come away with me. Tonight. I beg you!"

Alice's heart thumped uncontrollably. She was frozen like a petrified voyeur of another world in a distant time.

In anguish, the young woman shook her head, and the prince's expression changed. Anger exploded within him. He lunged towards the lady and ripped the pendant from around her neck.

"I gave you this!" he roared. "May the curse be on you, Alys! If I cannot have you, then neither shall my brother!"

He flung the charm against the castle wall and the ancient stone smashed in half. The terrified young woman stepped back towards the top of a winding staircase.

Alice cried out. A terrible pain cursed through her body. She opened her eyes and stumbled back against the barn wall.

"Alice! What is it? Are you all right?"

"Yes... I'm fine, Jean-Marc. I was just... er... day dreaming. I feel a little faint. It must be the heat."

"You look very pale. Do you want to sit down?"

"No. Really. I'm O.K. now."

Alice saw the small object in Jean-Marc's hand.

"What's that?"

"It's my stone."

Jean-Marc placed it on the table and Alice, still shaking, felt almost unable to resist as she took her own secret charm from the warmth of her pocket and laid it beside the other. They stared in silence.

"It's... well, they're both... do you think..." Alice looked at Jean-Marc in amazement. The young Frenchman bent over the stones and gently pushed them together.

"I can't see how it's possible, but when you look closely... yes, look here. Do you see?" Jean-Marc used his finger to trace across the two stones. "There's a wavy groove on my stone and it goes across onto yours if you arrange them this way."

Alice nodded. The groove did seem to continue across the two stones.

"Yes. Yes... it's as if they were once joined." She shiv-

23

ered. "Yours has a sharp edge on one side as if it has been broken. Mine doesn't though . . . unless its edge has been smoothed out somehow."

"Hum. I don't think so." Jean-Marc shook his head. "We must be crazy thinking they could once have been together. Where did you find yours again?"

"In my garden back home. It was just lying on the grass after the water went down."

"What water?"

"The river water. We live in Newark, quite near to the medieval castle and the River Trent. It flooded last winter and the water came right into our garden."

Jean-Marc shrugged his shoulders with indifference.

"The River Dordogne flooded last year too."

"Yeah . . . well. I suppose I'd better be getting back to the others before they miss me." Alice scooped her stone into her hand and plopped it into her pocket again. As she turned to climb back down the ladder she suddenly found herself wanting to ask Jean-Marc something silly.

"Could I borrow yours for a bit? I'll bring it back later."

For a moment, Jean-Marc looked reluctant to lose sight of his stone.

"Well . I suppose so. It's just a stone." He shrugged and put it in her hand. "You can bring it back tonight or tomorrow. Whenever you like."

"Thanks!" Alice beamed at him. She glanced at Jean-Marc's fossils. She would very much like to come back and examine the collection. "I've got to go!"

She descended the wooden ladder with ease, fled across the courtyard and ran up the drive as fast as she could. There was a rustle in the undergrowth above her and she looked up.

"Robert? Is that you?" But there was no one there.

As she rounded the corner of the drive, Alice slowed

down and sauntered towards the converted barns. Luckily the others were still gathering in front of the coach and the teachers didn't notice her join the back of the crowd. She felt in her pocket to check on the two stones and caught her breath for one terrible moment, until her fingers located a second unfamiliar shape with a slightly jagged edge. The two cold forms clanked gently together.

4

The First Journey

The coach ambled along the tree-lined avenues and the children gazed out at the rich tapestry of fields interrupted here and there by hamlets and castles and little roadside restaurants advertising their *Menu du Jour*.

"So? Where did you go?" asked Sarah, raising one eyebrow.

Alice wasn't sure about disclosing the whole truth to her friend.

"I found some yellow stones down the drive... and ...um, I had a little chat with our neighbours at the farmhouse. They wanted to know what part of England we were from." She smiled innocently at Sarah.

"Oh, yeah! Chinny, chin, chin! And did our *neighbours* bear any resemblance to that French boy you spoke to in the field last night... eh?" Sarah stroked her chin annoyingly. Alice could feel herself blushing.

"Maybe," she turned to look out of the window to hide her embarrassment.

"What's he like then? Are you going to introduce me?"

"He's not much fun..."

Sarah was giving Alice a look of complete disbelief.

"No... honestly, Sair. He's dead boring."

"I wish I could speak French like you, Alice. It's not fair!"

"It wouldn't make any difference. He's boring. Really, he is!"

The coach slowed down and pulled into a lay-by. Mr Hutchinson pointed across to the other side of the rocky canyon and the children got their first glimpse of the ramparts and roof tops of Rocamadour.

"Spectacular!" said Robert. "Cool castle!"

"Are those houses really cut out of the cliffs?" someone asked.

Miss Walton cleared her throat.

"The town is built on three levels. The castle is on the top, as you can see. Below it, half way down the cliff, is the twelfth century *Cité Religieuse*, which is a collection of chapels and crypts, and on the bottom is the town itself, with mostly shops and restaurants these days. Nowadays, we can use a lift to get from one part to another, but for centuries, the townspeople had to walk up hundreds of ancient steps, and thousands of pilgrims crawled up on their knees."

"I hope she doesn't expect us to do that!" whispered Robert, as he grimaced in mock pain towards his friend Luke.

"Does anyone know why pilgrims come to Rocamadour?" continued Miss Walton.

Tessa's hand shot up first.

"Yes, Tessa?"

"To see the relics, Miss Walton."

"Very good, Tessa. And what are relics?"

Everyone looked back at Tessa, but she remained silent, and went a little pink.

"Anybody?" Miss Walton looked around the class, but there were no volunteers.

"Well then, relics are old bones usually. In this case, the relics are thought to be the remains of the body of a saint that was unearthed close to the site of what is now the religious city, in ... er ..." She glanced down at her guidebook and continued to read from it. "Oh, yes ... , in the year 1166. At one time, this important pilgrimage site ranked alongside Rome and Jerusalem." She looked up. "There are supposed to have been many miracles here and many of our own English royalty have visited

27

the site. It was very popular in the time of the Crusades, I believe. In those days, of course, much of France was actually owned and ruled over by English kings and queens, like Richard the Lionheart, for example. Anyway, we're going to park up at the top by the castle."

Miss Walton, who was a French teacher, looked a little vexed after all that history. She glanced across at Mr Hutchinson, who obediently stood up.

"We'll have a look at the eagle sanctuary while we're up at the top, where we can have our packed lunch," said their form teacher. "We... oops!..."

At that moment the coach driver decided to start off again with a jolt, and Mr Hutchinson was thrown forward, almost landing in Miss Walton's long, bony lap. He steadied himself on the handrail and promptly sat down. The children made a very bad job of covering up their sniggers.

Alice, however, was not giggling with the rest. She was staring out of the window with a far away look on her face. A bird of prey soared high above the canyon and she followed it with her eyes. Inside her jeans pocket, she rubbed the two stones together between her fingers. She felt very strange and remote. The sounds of her noisy friends faded into the distance. Instead, she could hear the cries of the majestic bird as it climbed higher and higher above them. Suddenly, she jumped around as she heard a piercing woman's scream, which seemed to come from the seats behind. A horrible desire to be sick started to rise inside her, making her jaws shudder and she let go of her stones to bring her hands to her mouth. As she did so, the nausea faded and the chatter of her classmates grew louder again. She blinked hard and tried to focus her eyes. Robert and Luke were looking blankly at her from the seat behind.

"What's the matter? You look like you've seen a ghost!" said Robert.

"Are you feeling O.K.?" asked Sarah.

"I... er... yeah. I think so. Yes."

"Yes, what? Yes, you're O.K. or yes, you've seen a ghost?" laughed Luke.

"I'm not sure," said Alice, as she sat back down in her seat. She could still hear the terrible scream ringing in her ears, but at least she didn't feel sick anymore. She took out the two stones and held one in each hand, rubbing them absent-mindedly for unconscious re-assurance.

"Got another little pebble then?"

Alice sprang round. Robert was spying on her between the seats. She snapped her fingers shut.

The coach driver stopped the bus in the busy car park of Rocamadour and Mr Hutchinson and Miss Walton led the children down a rough path to the entrance of *Le Rocher des Aigles*. Once the tickets had been bought, they passed through the crowds and into the cliff top eagle sanctuary.

"Everybody, let's make our way towards the demonstration area. There is some kind of falconry display in ten minutes time. This way!" ordered Miss Walton.

"I liked the look of all those souvenir shops near the car park, didn't you!" said Sarah, as she pointed back towards the colourful displays of postcards, T-shirts and pottery.

Alice was feeling a bit better now. She felt in one of her pockets to make sure she had remembered her purse. She would be able to find some interesting gifts for her family here, as long as she could work out the prices. As she tugged at her little denim purse Jean-Marc's stone flew out onto the dusty ground.

"Oh, no!" she muttered in panic. As she leapt to retrieve it, Robert pushed her aside and swooped down to pick it up.

"That's mine! Give it back!"

29

"What's it worth?" sneered Robert. He turned his back on Alice and stole a look at the stone.

"It's not that exciting... but it feels cool and smooth, and I like this sharp edge..."

Robert casually rubbed the stone against the palm of his hand.

"Oh!"

A trickle of blood started to ooze from his skin.

"Please, Robert. Give me his stone back!"

"Whose stone?" asked Robert. He held the stone too high for Alice to reach. "Whose stone then?" he repeated, this time with a rather unpleasant smile across his face.

Alice didn't answer. She gave Robert a punch on the shoulder and held her hand out for the stone.

"Oooo! We are desperate, aren't we?" cooed Robert. "I bet it belongs to your French boyfriend, doesn't it?"

Alice looked surprised. Anger welled inside her.

"It's none of your business, Robert Davenport. Give it back, now, or I'll..."

"You'll what? Tell teacher on me? Oh, go on, then. Have your stupid stone back. It's got an ugly, sharp edge anyway. I could sue you, or your French friend, for causing me an injury!"

"Oh, shut up, idiot!" Alice snatched the stone from Robert's outstretched hand.

The jagged pebble tumbled into Alice's hand. As it jangled against her own stone, Alice began to feel sick and dizzy again. She stumbled forwards, falling into Robert's arms, and the two youngsters toppled over in a heap onto the stony ground.

An enormous, brown and white vulture cried loudly above their heads and came from nowhere to land heavily on it's sturdy, striding legs in the dust right in front of them. The huge bird flew so close that they found themselves ducking. If Alice hadn't been feeling sick, she would have laughed. She'd never been so close to a real bird of prey before and the landing had been quite spectacular, if a little comical.

"Wicked! It looks just like big planes when they come in to land, only bumpier."

The vulture waddled away, occasionally flapping its wings and Robert stood up. He coughed to clear the dust from his throat and looked down at Alice. In a rare moment of chivalry, he held out his hand and pulled her to her feet.

Just then, from somewhere behind them in a cloud of dust, they heard the unmistakable sound of a horse galloping at great speed towards them.

"It.... I... look out!" screamed Alice.

Just in time, they threw themselves against a court-yard wall as the horse and rider galloped furiously past. For several moments, neither spoke.

"There's something really weird going on," said Robert in a quiet voice. "Did you see the clothes that guy was wearing? He looked like a knight straight out of a med-ieval film or something! I'm sure he was wearing bits of armour. And did you see that shield with the red and gold coat of arms?"

"Yes. I did," said Alice. "Cor! It really stinks around here now!" She wrinkled up her nose.

"Yeah. Like someone didn't flush the toilet properly! Hey... where have all the others gone?"

The two children started looking around them. There was nobody in sight. The low barns where the eagles and buzzards had been were gone. They were standing in an enclosed courtyard in front of a wooden dwelling of some sort. There were a couple of pigs snuffling in the dirt and chickens everywhere. Across the courtyard from the house was a rough barn that housed a sleepy looking brown cow. Two horses were tethered to an outside rail and the drapery under each saddle was emblazoned with the same bright red coat of arms they had seen on the galloping rider's shield. Three golden lions were embroidered down the centre.

Suddenly, a door in the house flew open and two women ran out. The first was a young lady wearing a long cloak over a velvet dress. She quickly reached one of the horses and drew her hood over her blond hair as she waited for the older, rather plump servant woman to catch her up.

The servant, who was sobbing loudly, knelt down and allowed her mistress to use her cupped hands as a step to saddle the horse sideways.

"You should not be going yourself, my Lady Clare," she puffed. "This should not be the task of a lady-in-waiting. Where is Prince John? He said HE would bring this holy man himself ... this *seer*... here to Rocamadour to heal my poor Lady Alys. Why has Prince John deserted her?" Alice recognised the language as French with an unusual accent.

"John is in grave danger," said Lady Clare. "He must retreat to England. But he has sent word. He has told me where to find the seer. His squire and I will swiftly return with him. Don't worry..." She glanced in the direction of the house. "All will be well."

In a flash, the cloaked lady drove the horse into a canter and the beast and rider clattered past the bewildered children.

"Make haste, my Lady!" cried the servant woman. "May God speed you in your purpose!"

Alice and Robert looked at each other in astonishment.

"I did hear a scream," muttered Alice.

"A scream? When?" Robert looked at her blankly.

"On the coach. I heard this desperate scream. I felt sick, just like a minute ago, and I smelt horses and leather. There's a connection, I know it." Alice started to

32

walk towards the sobbing lady.

"Excusez moi, Madame!" She broke into a run, but the servant did not acknowledge her. "Hello! Excuse me! Can you tell me where we are?"

Alice was directly in front of the woman, yet still she was ignored.

"Hello! What has happened here?"

Alice tried again, first in English, then in French, but the plump servant woman in brown medieval robes just stared straight through Alice into the distance, in the direction of the fleeing horses.

Robert had recovered now. He ran over to Alice.

"Maybe she's deaf," he suggested, and he reached out to touch the woman's arm. "Aaargh!"

As he got within an inch of her flesh, he recoiled in pain.

"My arm!"

As the woman turned to go back into the house, Alice tried to grab her, and she too felt a deep burning through her hand and up her arm.

"It's as if we're not here!" she cried through clenched teeth.

"Let's follow her!" said Robert.

After a minute's hesitation, the two youngsters gingerly climbed some stone steps and entered the dim structure. As she passed through the doorway, Alice touched the thick doorframe.

"Well, the door's real at any rate, and I can smell proper smells."

Just then, a young servant girl rushed within an arm's reach of Alice and Robert.

"Oy!" called Robert boldly, but the girl carried on by.

"Let's look in here, I can hear a voice," said Alice in slightly hushed tones, as she crept through a low doorway.

"I don't know why you're whispering. Nobody seems to

33

be able to see or hear us," said Robert. "Where are we? What's happened to us, Alice?"

As the two children entered the dimly lit room, they found it difficult to adjust to the darkness. The window had been firmly shuttered and the only light came from two wax candles and the flickering of a smoky fire. A heavy bed stood against the far wall. The tall, curved wood at both the head and the foot of the bed made it look like a Viking boat. The plump woman knelt down and began to pray.

The smoke was thick and irritant in Robert's unaccustomed throat and he was forced to retreat into the outer chamber to cough violently. Alice thought she could see a dark-haired woman lying motionless under the bedclothes. She tried to listen to what the older woman was saying.

"Dear Lord, protect my Lady Clare on her journey to bring the seer to heal my Lady Alys."

The servant turned her tearstained face to stare fondly at the young woman lying motionless on the bed, whose noble features were framed by locks of long, ebony black hair.

"My poor Lady Alys," continued the servant, shaking her head. "Those Plantagenet princes are nothing but a pair of rogues! You are Alys of France... King Philip's sister! So clever and beautiful. So gracious and kind. Oh, why did your father ever betroth you to that evil Richard! Why should you carry the duty to marry an English king? That won't stop his warmongering... or his people starving to pay his taxes!"

Alice's eyes grew wide in amazement as she began to understand. She looked more closely at the woman in the bed and gasped as she recognised her as the lady with the pendant she had dreamed about earlier. The old woman's mutterings continued, more angrily now.

"See, my Lady! Even your beloved John has run back to

England. He has betrayed you after almost killing you. Oh, he may say you fell by accident down all those steps in the castle tower... but he's to blame... that Prince John! And to think you almost ran away with him! Still, you might have escaped Richard's bullying then, at least! How you've kept smiling amazes me after he's kept you prisoner in his castles for so long, while he goes off fighting with infidels. Look at you, my poor, doomed Alys of France!"

5

Theories of Time Travel

Alice started to feel very sick and shaky again. Her head was whirling with ideas and possibilities. Could she really have travelled back in time to the Middle Ages? Somehow, this injured lady was connected to King Richard and Prince John. Then she realised. The man she'd seen in her dream... the one pacing around the castle chamber! That must have been John... and he was really angry. He'd pulled the stone pendant from the lady's neck. Did the lady... this lady now lying in front of her... did she then fall back down the stairs?

"But that wasn't here, in Rocamadour," said Alice under her breath. "And there's something else familiar... a connection somewhere. Oh, what is it?" She started to cough.

"Robert! Rob..." she managed to shout in between splutters. Robert's form emerged from the smoke and darkness.

"What is it? Alice! Alice, where are you? Oh, there you are. Urgh! I feel really sick again... Hey! You look all weird."

Alice could just see Robert in the shadows, but he was looking fainter and almost transparent. In panic, she grabbed for his hand.

In the next moment, they found themselves falling to the dusty floor on top of one another again, but now their heads were spinning with the chaotic noise of children's voices all around them, and the screetch-screetching of large birds very close by.

"Robert Davenport, what do you think you are doing! Stop pushing Alice around! Sit up! Now! Quickly, or

36

you will miss your turn!"

Robert rubbed his eyes and tried to do what Miss Walton's irate voice was asking. As both he and Alice sat up straight, they found themselves in the ridiculous situation of sitting with their legs out in a long ladder of children while an eagle trainer led a waddling vulture by the wing as it strode across their legs. Its claws were only a little sharp. They tickled really. After the bird of prey had passed on by to walk over other children's knees, Robert and Alice looked at each other, and for some reason they burst into uncontrollable laughter.

The two friends spent most of lunchtime discussing their adventure. While the others were exchanging views on what it felt like to have a vulture walk on your knees, or the other showpiece of having an eagle standing on your head, Robert was listening to Alice's theories of how they had somehow travelled back in time.

"We both believe it, don't we?" she checked with her new partner in the mystery, while stuffing the last of a Camembert cheese sandwich into her mouth.

"Yep. We went back in time somehow," nodded Robert, swigging lemonade. It was the hottest part of the day, and they were glad of the shade under the trees.

"But how?" said Alice. "We didn't go through a doorway or enter any kind of machine. None of it really seems to make sense. By the way, you never saw the lady on the bed did you? And did you hear what the servant lady was saying?"

"No. I didn't realise you had. Come on, then. What?"

Alice recounted what the servant had said as accurately as she could remember. Then she told Robert about her dream.

"Wow! Richard the Lionheart's fiancée knocked down the castle steps by Prince John! Nah! Couldn't be...

could it?"

Alice just shrugged.

"I felt sick too, you know, just before we got there," continued Robert. "And just as we came back. Better watch it if you feel sick again!"

"Do you think it might happen again?" Alice said in alarm.

"How should I know. I don't know how it happened that time, do I!"

"Well, let's think back. What were we doing just beforehand?" asked Alice. Robert looked guiltily at her, waiting for her to remember. "Oh, yes. You'd taken my stones." She looked crossly at him, although her anger was less now that they had shared something secret and powerful together.

"Not both your stones, I think," corrected Robert, "It's his, isn't it, the other one. It belongs to that French boy whose house you went to this morning."

"Yes. O.K. So it's Jean-Marc's."

"Oh, that's his name, is it?" Robert looked irritated.

"Hang on. I . . . yes, that has to be it . . ."

A feeling of fearful excitement started to rise inside Alice.

"The stones!" she breathed. "It's when they're together!"

Carefully she took out her own stone and laid it on the grass next to the cling film from her sandwich. Then she felt in her other pocket and produced Jean-Marc's. She laid that one down some distance away. They didn't look very exciting. They were a rather boring bronzy yellow colour, speckled with grey flecks that sparkled slightly in the sunlight. Alice's stone was smoother and more polished, while the surface of Jean-Marc's was slightly pitted in places. Across them both ran a wavy groove. The more she looked, the more certain Alice was that they had once been united as a single stone which had somehow broken in half. Alice explained to Robert how she found hers washed up in her own garden, back in England, and that Jean-Marc found his in an ancient wall in his farmhouse. Neither of them dared to put the two stones right next to each other.

"It's all a bit far fetched isn't it? How could your half have found it's way to Newark-on-Trent?" said Robert at last. "Yet, there does seem to be a connection. It was when they were together in your hand, wasn't it?"

"Yes, just like on the coach when I heard the scream. I wonder if it was the injured lady's scream as she fell? Do you think there really was an Alys of France? Oh, it all seems so ridiculous! Nobody would believe us!" Alice was beginning to think she was going crazy. She looked at Robert, who was deep in thought. He'd been there too though, so it must have been real.

"If we were at home," Alice continued, trying to convince herself that it did really happen, "we could look up that red and gold coat of arms in the library and check up on the history."

Robert grinned. "Would the internet do?"

They looked at each other and spoke simultaneously: "Miss Walton's lap top!"

For the rest of the afternoon, Alice and Robert were only half interested in what was going on around them. They were both so excited about the possibilities of their plans. They would ask Miss Walton if they could borrow her computer to do some research for their project.

The two of them drifted through the guided tour of the *Chapel de Notre Dame,* although they were briefly distracted by the tale of the Black Madonna, who's ninth century bell was said to ring on it's own when a miracle was about to occur.

After walking down the famous staircase used by the pilgrims, the children were allowed to spend half an hour buying souvenirs and delicious French ice cream in the myriad of little shops that had long since taken over the whole of the ancient main street of Rocamadour.

"Now, I vote we make tracks back to *La Grange*, to allow time for an hour's project work before a cooling dip in the swimming pool, don't you agree?"

Miss Walton had calculated well. The mention of the swimming pool brought a cheer of approval.

"Alice, are you going to sit next to me on the way back, or loverboy over there?" asked Sarah, sarcastically. She was pointing at Robert who was busy admiring the rocks with his friend Luke, through the clear sides of the funicular lift capsule as it transported them slowly up the sheer face of the cliff.

"Of course I'll sit with you, Sair! Hey, I'm sorry I got a bit bogged down with Robert, but he's NOT my loverboy. We just had this idea about a project, that's all."

6

A Curse on Robert

They were soon back at *La Grange aux Fleurs*.
"Right, settle down everyone," said Miss
Walton. "Before we outline how to go about your project for the week, you'll be interested to know that the weather back home is awful. It hasn't stopped raining heavily in Newark since we left. The Trent is on full flood alert again. Unfortunately, the weather forecast for this part of France is not good for the second half of the week either. Unusually, there is a strong probability of heavy rain in this area, and the rivers hereabout might also flood. It seems the floods are following us like a curse! Better make the most of the outdoor swimming pool in the next day or so."

For some reason, Alice felt that shivery feeling again, and for a brief moment she felt slightly sick. She checked for the bulges in her pockets, and both were still there. Then she looked across at Robert and found him looking back at her. He mouthed something about the computer and pointed at the teacher. Miss Walton was speaking again.

". . . so, you can get straight in the pool, or sunbathe. Whatever you like. Oh, yes, and two of you have asked if you can work together and if you may use the portable computer. Working in pairs is absolutely fine, and the suggestion about the computer is an excellent one. Well done Robert and Alice! You two may go on the computer first, after supper. I'll draw up a rota for the rest of you to fill in, if you also wish to use it."

Alice grinned at Robert who winked back. Then she

41

glanced across at Tessa to see her glaring furiously, first at Robert and then at her.

The swimming pool was sensational. The clear water lapped over their hot bodies in delicious velvet waves. Alice and Sarah took turns to throw their goggles in the deep end for the other one to retrieve in ten seconds, timed on Sarah's waterproof watch. Robert, Luke and some of the other boys were playing a similar game with coins.

"Bet the girls could get them quicker!" challenged Alice.

The boys laughed scornfully.

"If you let us use your stop-watch, we'll find out, won't we!" retaliated one of the boys.

"You're on!" cried the girls at once. "Us first. Give us the coins!"

The happy youngsters continued with their noisy battle, shouting at the opposition and collapsing into taunting laughter. The water glittered and splashed in the golden warmth of the French evening, amid the rhythmic chirping of the cicadas. A mouth-watering smell of spit-roasted chicken wafted temptingly from the direction of the dining barn.

"That's it! I've had it!" gasped Robert, as he hauled himself out and dripped his way across to the pile of towels on the little wall that surrounded the pool.

One at a time, the others followed, and they sat on the wall or the grass, wrapped in their colourful beach towels. There were no sun-loungers left. Tessa and her crowd had occupied most of them, with their books and towels strewn obstructively on any empty ones. Alice flicked her sopping hair over the top of her head and leant back with her face to the sun.

"If I don't get some food soon, I'll faint," she said.

"I've got some French chocolate in my bag that I bought earlier," said Sarah. "D'ya fancy some?"

"I do!" interrupted Robert.

Just as Alice was about to agree to the idea, the meal gong sounded.

"After!" she whispered, as they all sprang to their feet and headed off towards the wonderful smell.

Mr Hutchinson appeared in the doorway.

"Oh, no you don't! Not in those wet costumes! You'd better put some dry things on double quick!"

Tessa, who hadn't got wet, had slipped her shorts on top of her dry costume.

"Excuse me, please," she said, pushing past Alice and Sarah. "Ummm! Doesn't that chicken smell good!" she added venomously.

Alice stuck her tongue out behind Tessa's back and ran off to get changed as quickly as possible.

Supper was delicious again. Well, Alice thought so. Some of the others thought the olives were disgusting, but everyone liked the chunks of warm *baguette* and most people went up for seconds of the chicken. Madame Magret was carving rough slices of hot meat straight from the joints as fast as her husband could get them off the giant barbecue spits behind them.

"Merci, Madame," said Alice.

"Comment t'appelles-tu?" asked the French woman. She was a slim, smiley lady with dark eyes and nearly black hair. She had very brown skin and was wearing a simple, short flowery dress with a sleeveless navy blue apron coat buttoned over the top.

"Je m'appelle Alice."

They continued chatting in French.

"Ah, yes. I thought so. You have a very good accent. My son told me that there was one among you who spoke such good French. He said you have family nearby?"

Miss Walton sidled up and tried to get in on the conversation.

43

"She speaks the language well, doesn't she?" ventured the teacher in her less convincing staccato French with a heavy English accent.

Madame Magret smiled a little stiffly back. At that moment, Jean- Marc appeared around the barn door. He spotted Alice and took his mother to one side. Alice could feel a little colour creeping annoyingly into her cheeks.

Someone cleared his throat behind Alice's shoulder and she turned round to face Robert. He raised his eyebrows at her and glared menacingly.

"Don't forget we have to use that computer after supper," he whispered.

"Madamoiselle Walton," said the French woman, speaking in English now. "My son has apparently been helping Alice with her work and she needs to come over to the farmhouse for more information from his collection. She can come over now? It is agreeable to me."

"Oh, well, I'm not sure..." Miss Walton seemed a little thrown by the suggestion.

"I'll go too," offered Robert, looking pleadingly at his teacher. "Do you have a computer?" he asked Jean-Marc.

Jean-Marc looked at Alice, then shrugged, nodding.

"Please, Miss Walton?" said Robert.

"Well, I don't know. It seems very rude..."

"*Mais non*. Not at all," said Madame Magret. "It's up to you, of course."

"Well, ... I suppose so. But you must be back by nine o'clock. Is that clear?"

"Thank you, Miss Walton!" replied Robert and Alice in unison, and before anyone could change their minds, they all ran out of the barn.

"Wicked!" laughed Robert, as they fled down the driveway. "Hi! My name's Rob. I know yours. Alice will have to translate if we can't understand each other."

Jean-Marc nodded his agreement. "I can speak some English," he replied with a cautious smile. They slowed down and the two boys shook hands.

"How did you get on in Rocamadour, then?" Jean-Marc asked Alice.

"Ah, well, there's something we need to tell you ..." "She looked across at Robert, and he nodded in agreement. "It's about the stones ... "

Alice and Robert took turns to recount their peculiar experience at the eagle sanctuary, with Alice attempting to translate any bits that Jean-Marc couldn't understand. He listened, and shook his head from time to time, in disbelief.

"We'll have to try again, Alice. I want to go back," said Robert. They were about to climb the ladder to Jean-Marc's loft.

Alice was silent. She felt suddenly afraid.

"I don't want to," she said. "I think we're playing about with something very powerful."

"Can I have my stone back?" asked Jean-Marc.

"Oh, yes. Of course," said Alice. She felt in her shorts pocket and withdrew one stone in each hand. Nobody spoke. They all gazed at the small, ordinary looking rocks in Alice's hands.

Then suddenly, Robert snatched them both.

"Hey!" cried Alice.

"Give them back!" shouted Jean-Marc. He took a menacing step forwards.

Robert stood in front of them. He had one stone in each hand, but his hands were very close together. He looked at the others with a challenging sneer on his face. There was malice in Robert's expression that Alice had never seen before. He seemed bigger and more powerful now. She felt uneasy. Something was wrong. Robert seemed possessed by an evil force and as the others watched, he deliberately closed his hands together.

"No!" yelled Alice.

Just in time, Jean-Marc and Alice leapt forward on top of him.

7

Death by the Sword

Alice recognised the nauseous feeling from before, although it was not so bad this time and she knew that everything would be different even before she started to examine her surroundings more closely. Jean-Marc was still sitting on the ground, looking rather peaky. His familiar farmhouse home had vanished. Instead, they were in the dining hall of a castle.

A long wooden table spanned one end of the room, with platters and goblets strewn haphazardly on top and two narrower tables stretched away from it along the length of the hall. These had benches on either side, unlike the top table, which had high-backed thrones for the most important banquet guests. An enormous central hearth was set in the floor and a blazing fire crackled and spat, sending swirls of smoke to find their way out through the open rafters in the high ceiling. Two slender hunting dogs dozed in front of the fire.

The sound of distant voices filtered through one of the doorways. Jean-Marc stood up, gaping around him in disbelief. As he did so, the two dogs sat up. One of them gave a low, warning growl and then a single bark. The children jumped.

"Can they see us?" whispered Alice, but the dog dropped his head onto his paws and closed his eyes again.

"I'm not sure," said Robert nervously. "Maybe they can smell us. Let's edge around to that door. I don't think I fancy going too close to them just in case."

"Of course they can't see us, silly! They're hunting

dogs. If they knew we were here they'd be on us by now," said Jean-Marc. Robert didn't look convinced.

Keeping their eyes on the dogs, the children shuffled around the tables to an arched doorway. Once or twice one of the dogs opened his eyes, but he didn't lift his head again. They reached a small round outer chamber. A winding staircase stretched from the stone floor to the barrel-vaulted ceiling high above.

Suddenly, there were footsteps at the top of the stairs. They froze against the wall. If they had been visible, they would surely have been in full view to the two people on the steps but to the children's surprise, the man and the woman walked straight past them without a flicker of recognition.

They were dressed in medieval robes. The young lady's velvet dress was a rich, dark green and was heavily embroidered. The man wore a brown leather tunic and a belt with an ornately crafted buckle. On every finger he wore a jewelled ring and despite his youth, he had the bearing and authority of someone born into the ranks of nobility. Alice recognised him immediately.

"I will fetch the seer. It is her only hope!" said the man. "You must do what you can here."

"But my Lord, she has asked to go to Rocamadour. It is her wish. We could smuggle her out tonight. The king will not know... and neither will he care." The last remark was said with hatred.

"My Lady Clare, there is magic to deal with here, an ancient curse, from the Age of the Cave Dwellers. It is the stone. Now it is broken, it is as the seer said... my beloved Alys is dying..."

Prince John faltered as he pulled one half of the smashed stone pendant from his pocket and rolled it over in his fingers. He jerked it away again. Lady Clare watched him.

"Believe me, my Lady. I have witnessed the power of

this curse before. You can only fight magic with magic. I will bring the seer to her. His ways are more certain. There is no truth in what they say about Rocamadour."

"No, I beg you my Lord. We must do her bidding!"

The young woman fell to her knees. Her voice became quieter.

"She is dying from her injuries, my Lord John! If you love her, you will honour her last wishes."

For a moment, the man did not reply. He looked up towards the top of the winding castle staircase.

"Oh... very well, move her! My squire will deal with the king's guards and escort you to the inn at Rocamadour. I will try to bring the seer there. It will be dangerous though. My enemies are everywhere. If Richard returns, he may try to kill me... but I suppose there is virtue in that he will not find Alys at Rocamadour. She will be safe there. I will send word if there is trouble and tell you what to do. Go now. Make haste!"

The lady rose to her feet and kissed the hand of the young prince, before fleeing up the stairs. His troubled face watched after her for a few moments before he passed into the hall towards the dogs.

"Shall we follow him?" whispered Alice.

"Maybe we should," said Robert. "Hang on... someone's coming back down. Sshhh!"

There were bumping sounds of something heavy being carried down the stairs. They looked up. Robert and Alice glanced at each other as they recognised the squire. He was the rider who had almost run them down in Rocamadour. He was supporting the front of a primitive wooden stretcher while Lady Clare struggled with the other end. A young woman lay motionless under a blanket on the stretcher.

"Lady Alys of France!" murmured Alice.

The puffing squire stumbled suddenly. Jean-Marc,

who was the closest of the three, instinctively rushed forward to try to help him, and put his shoulder under the side of the stretcher, temporarily taking its weight. The man recovered his footing and looked up at Lady Clare in confusion, surprised at her ability to control the stretcher alone.

"They can't see Jean-Marc," whispered Robert.

The squire stepped almost against the wall to allow Lady Clare to rotate her end around the post at the foot of the staircase. Jean-Marc let go and ducked under the stretcher just in time to avoid being crushed.

"Jean-Marc!" gasped Alice. But the young Frenchman rolled out from under the wood and sprang back up to his feet.

Robert reached out and brushed his hand against the side of the wood. He smiled, but then, as his hand fell to within an inch of Lady Clare, he recoiled in pain.

"Aaaah! She's so hot or something!"

"Did you feel the stretcher?" asked Alice.

"Yes. But not her. It was like electricity again."

"We can touch things, but not people," said Alice.

Jean-Marc was watching the figures in the dining hall. The dogs and Prince John had gone.

The other two gently placed the stretcher on to the top table while they fastened their cloaks. They exchanged a few hurried words before the lady took a deep breath and approached the outer door. The squire drew his sword. With a jerk, Lady Clare opened the door and started to scream and a moment later, two unsuspecting guards rushed in.

In horror, Alice raised her hands to her mouth as the squire drove his shining blade into the chest of the first man. The second guard drew his sword and engaged the squire in deadly combat. The blades clashed and sparked. The guard lunged towards his adversary, but the squire had anticipated the attack and he deftly parried his opponent's blade and his reposte pierced the other's chain mail tunic with fatal accuracy. The guard fell dying to the floor in a growing pool of blood.

Robert, Alice and Jean-Marc were paralysed with terror.

"Quick, my Lady! We must hurry!" shouted the squire, as the two of them reached for the ends of the stretcher and bundled it through the door to the courtyard beyond.

The three watchers did not move. For several awful minutes, the children stared at the guards' crumpled bodies.

The sound of cart wheels on the wet cobbles outside brought them to their senses. They peered out into the pouring rain and were in time to see the squire whipping the horses on. They could just make out the hooded silhouette of Lady Clare through the flapping curtains of the carriage window as she bent over Lady Alys cradled in her arms.

The red coat of arms with three gold lions was painted on the carriage door. As the horses clattered past, splashing water in all directions, a small piece of stone fell from the carriage step and skimmed across the courtyard away from the children. Alice recognised it at once. It was the other half of the stone pendant that Prince John had smashed in rage.

"Half of one whole... just like... Jean-Marc's and mine... surely not...!" The stone fragment rolled away towards the ancient courtyard wall. At once, she knew she was right.

She felt a surge of power course through her like a massive shiver. Instinctively, she felt in her pocket. To her surprise, her pocket was empty. In panic, she turned her other pocket inside out. Then she remembered. Robert had the stones. Alice turned towards where Robert had been standing, but he had vanished. She

51

wheeled round and raced back into the castle hall, followed closely by Jean-Marc.

"There you are! What are you doing?"

Robert had picked up the sword of one of the dead guards and he was waving it about, practicing fencing movements in the air. He had that unpleasant look on his face again.

"Idiot!" exclaimed Jean-Marc. "You are behaving like a madman! Are you possessed by evil spirits or something?"

"He's got the stones. If they are cursed, maybe they're affecting him too," said Alice.

Robert bounced up on top of a table and began advancing and retreating along his wooden stage. He grinned viciously and lunged forward.

"Et la!" he shouted triumphantly as his weapon vanquished his invisible foe. Then, for some reason, he dropped the heavy weapon and gripped his stomach.

"What's the matter? Cut yourself accidentally have you?" scoffed Jean-Marc.

"He's looking faded. I can almost see through him... oh, no ... he's going back, Jean-Marc. Quick! Hold my hand!"

8

A Clue in Heraldry

Alice leapt onto the table using the bench as a stepping stone, and dragged Jean-Marc towards a rapidly fading Robert. They threw themselves on top of him and fell, once again, into a nauseating swirl of matter.

With a thud, they landed in a heap. They were no longer on the old oak table but were back on the floor of Jean-Marc's den.

It was getting dark.

"Wow! That was amazing, wasn't it?" said Robert, grinning triumphantly.

"I want my stone back, please," asked Alice as politely as she could, holding her hand out towards him.

Robert looked at her unpleasantly and stood up slowly. He wasn't smiling anymore. Jean-Marc's eyes narrowed. He took a step towards Robert, but the English boy did not volunteer to surrender their property. His hands remained firmly in his pockets. Alice and Jean-Marc were between him and the ladder, blocking his escape. Robert's eyes flicked around him taking in the collection of fossils, stones and teeth.

"Cool stuff, Jean. Can I see?"

He edged closer to the bookshelves.

"Don't try and distract us. Give back what's not yours! And my name is Jean-MARC, not Jean."

"Jean... John... whatever!" sneered Robert.

Alice shook her head in disbelief. Robert was so different since he had possessed the stones.

Outside, they heard the whining engine of a moped pulling up nearby.

"Pascal, my brother! Go and get him Alice. Quick!" hissed Jean-Marc under his breath in rapid French. Alice didn't hesitate and in no time, she was down the ladder. She ran straight across the courtyard towards the older boy. He looked very like Jean-Marc with the same dark eyes and skin, but he wore his long hair in a pony tail.

"Qu'est-ce que c'est?"

"Hi! Your brother's in trouble!" panted Alice, in French. "He needs you in the den. He sent me to get you. There's this other boy..."

But Jean-Marc's older brother was already sprinting back towards the open-fronted barn ahead of her. Alice could now hear the two boys fighting in the loft above. Dust fell from the platform as she climbed the ladder after Pascal.

"Oh, no!" she exclaimed.

The two boys were wrestling aggressively on the floor. The bookshelves had been knocked over and Jean-Marc's collection was strewn all around. Although shorter, Robert was the more aggressive of the two and he pinned Jean-Marc to the floor. Pascal waded into the fight and grabbed Robert from behind in an arm lock, dragging him to his feet.

"Owww! Let me go you ... arghhhh!"

Jean-Marc landed an unpleasant looking punch in Robert's stomach.

"Hold him still!" Jean-Marc ordered his brother in French. "He's got something that doesn't belong to him!"

Jean-Marc felt in Robert's pockets and extracted first his own stone and then Alice's. He was careful to keep them apart as he passed Alice's back to her. She rammed it safely into her own pocket.

"Thanks, Pascal. That's it. It's finished. You can let him go."

There was a rapid interchange of dialogue between

the two brothers. Robert slumped to the floor, nursing his bruises and eyed the two of them warily. He looked small and deflated now, and slightly ashamed. Pascal, satisfied that Robert no longer presented a threat, retreated down the ladder.

"I won't be far away. Shout if you need me again," he added as he disappeared.

"You idiot!" said Alice to Robert in disgust. "Whatever came over you? You were so different."

"Are you going to apologise?" Jean-Marc demanded, in English again.

There was an awkward pause.

"Yeah, well, I just got a bit carried away or something."

"That's not an apology!"

"O.K. O.K. I'm sorry, all right?"

"No, it's not all right. You went berserk back there," said Alice. "And you should never have used the stones, our stones, in the first place!"

Alice was beginning to feel less angry with Robert now. He looked more like his usual self again, instead of the wild maniac of earlier.

"Exactly where were we? That's what I'd like to know," said Robert, changing the subject.

Alice sat down on the edge of the old armchair. She gave a long sigh and surveyed the mess on the floor.

"We were going to look up that coat of arms on the computer, but it's getting dark and we'll have to clear this mess up, won't we?" she said.

"Yes. All right. All right," muttered Robert. "Is your brother going to tell your parents?" he asked Jean-Marc sheepishly.

"No. I told him to keep quiet about it for the moment. If you put this lot back, I'll sneak back inside to my computer and see if I can find anything out. Alice, will you be all right here with him? You'd better keep an eye on him in case he pinches anything," he said scornfully.

Alice looked at Robert.

"Yeah, I'll be fine. Go on. Don't be too long though. We'd better go back soon, before they send out a search party."

Robert watched as Alice smiled reassuringly at Jean-Marc. Her blue eyes were shining. Jean-Marc shot a final warning glance at Robert before descending the ladder and setting off towards his house.

"I'm really sorry, Alice. I can't explain it. Look, I'll get this lot back on the shelf in no time... and I promise I won't take anything. I'm not a thief. I just wanted to borrow the stones." He jumped to his feet and started picking things up.

"I was a bit surprised, Rob. What happened to you? What were you going to do... go back again?"

"I dunno. Really, I don't know anymore. I wasn't myself. That bloke back then... Prince John... he talked about some kind of magic didn't he? What did he call it... a curse?"

"Yes. He said he was going to fetch a *seer*. Maybe a seer was some kind of magic man in those days. Maybe a seer can undo curses. I don't know. I'm just guessing," Alice said, thinking aloud.

She paused from helping to pick up the fallen treasures and stared absent-mindedly into the air in front of her. She was seeing again the lovely green velvet dress and the anxious face of the woman called Lady Clare and smelling the strong, unfamiliar smells of what was probably the medieval castle that had once stood here. She heard again the clatter of cart wheels on wet cobbles and felt the warm rain on her face and arms. She flinched as she reluctantly heard that piercing scream again, and the clash of the sharp blades of heavy swords in combat.

She was startled back to the present by Jean-Marc's voice as he appeared at the top of the ladder once more.

He looked triumphant.

"I've got it! I found it! It was easy. I just typed in 'coats of arms' and the first site I hit had the exact one, right at the beginning. Look... I printed it out!"

Jean-Marc spread the piece of paper on the table and the others looked at the drawing of a shield in front of them. It was bright red with three golden lions on it.

Alice translated the French caption that was underneath the shield:

"The Royal Arms of Richard the Lionheart, King of England 1189-1199."

"Wow! What else does it say?" said Robert.

"It's all here... yes... Alys of France," Alice grinned with excitement. "Sister of King Philip of France, betrothed to Prince Richard and sent to live in the English court of King Henry on her eighth birthday."

"Does it say what became of her?" asked Jean-Marc.

"No. But she didn't marry Richard. He married someone else... and it looks as if he died soon after."

"Did Alys die then?" asked Robert.

"I don't think we'll ever know... it doesn't say any more about her."

9

A Plan is Made

The morning sky was clear and blue again as Alice emerged after a restless night. Lizards flitted and darted over the warm stones and a pair of dragon-flies hovered near the honeysuckle growing up the barn walls. Alice lifted her face towards the bright sun. Dogs barked in the distance and she heard the occasional aeroplane, like a rumble of distant thunder. A fly buzzed loudly past her head.

She walked over towards the hum of the swimming pool intending to investigate the water filters for any trapped frogs.

"Hello. You're up early too," came a voice from behind her at the side of the barn.

Robert was sitting at the edge of the pond, poking it with a stick. He looked thoughtfully at Alice with a slight smile in his blue eyes.

"Yeah. Couldn't sleep. Like you, by the looks of it."

Alice sat down and watched the scurrying tadpoles.

"You want to go back, don't you?" she said.

"Don't you?"

"I suppose so. It was amazing. But you were an idiot you know. I don't want to go with you if you're going to behave like a pratt..."

"I know! I know! I've said I'm sorry, haven't I?"

Robert got up and brushed the dirt from his jeans.

"We have to go back! Who knows where we might get to next..."

"Exactly!"

They heard someone approaching.

"There you are, Alice. Breakfast is ready you know," said Sarah.

Alice smiled at her and got up. She thought Sarah was looking a bit fed up, so she made conversation about writing the postcards they'd bought in Rocamadour.

During breakfast, Mr Hutchinson outlined the plans for the day. They were going to visit a troglodyte city and see how people lived in rock caves through the ages, especially in the Stone Age. He explained that people who lived in caves were called troglodytes. Alice had visited some of the pre-historic parks in the area before and had seen cave paintings of horses and bison, but she never tired of looking at them. She dreamed of one day finding some real archeological treasures for herself.

Suddenly, it occurred to her that with the stones, she might be able to go back to pre-historic times, although she didn't fancy meeting any cave bears or mountain lions. She would dearly love to see a woolly mammoth though. She began to feel really excited. Her eyes met Robert's. Somehow she knew he was thinking the same thing.

But it was her stone, and Jean-Marc owned the other one. She wasn't sure she wanted Robert to keep joining in. On the other hand, she didn't fancy trying to use the stones on her own very much. She made up her mind to try and sneak off to find Jean-Marc after breakfast.

As it happened, the young Frenchman appeared with his mother to help clear up the breakfast things. Alice picked up her empty plate and bowl and walked over towards Jean-Marc.

"I need to talk to you," she whispered. "Can you meet me behind the barn?"

He nodded slightly. Alice deposited her dirty crockery and confidently headed out of the barn and up the slope outside, hoping Robert hadn't seen her. A minute later, Jean-Marc appeared round the corner.

Alice began to explain her idea of travelling back even further in time.

"Hold on just a minute, Alice. How could you be sure you'd end up in any particular period in time? You could end up face-to-face with a dinosaur!"

For a second, Alice's eyes sparkled at that prospect, but her common sense suggested that experiencing dinosaurs first hand might not be such a good idea.

"That wouldn't happen, anyway," she said.

"Why not? I don't think we have any control over these stones."

"No. But maybe they have control over us."

"What's that supposed to mean?"

"I'm not sure, exactly. But I think we'll be O.K. Don't ask me how, but I think you and I were meant to find each other, and the stones. Our stones are the two halves of the stone pendant I saw around Lady Alys' neck. I think the stones are taking us exactly where they want us to go for some reason. It's got something to do with the curse, and Alys of France, and King Richard, and Prince John. What was it John said ... an ancient curse from the Age of the Cave Dwellers? I've got a feeling about the troglodyte city..."

"Woah! Slow down, Alice!" laughed Jean-Marc. "You can't be sure of any of this."

Alice was breathing very fast as she considered the possibilities. Her blue, intelligent eyes shone with certainty.

"There's a big problem though," she said.

Jean-Marc raised one eyebrow.

"How did my half of the stone get into my garden in England?"

They both shrugged and looked at each other for a moment.

Then Alice clapped her hands with delight.

"Of course! Newark Castle!"

"I don't understand. What about it?"

"He went there. He DIED there!"

"Who did?"

"John, idiot! Prince John. Only he was king by then... King of England. What if he kept his half of the stone, and took it with him always, because he loved Alys?"

"Ahh! How romantic."

Alice gave Jean-Marc a 'you're so pathetic' stare.

"Doesn't explain how it got in your garden though."

"Uhmmn." Alice slumped down.

They were silent again.

"The Age of the Cave Dwellers, eh?" mused Jean-Marc. "Maybe I can come with you... to the troglodyte city?"

"But how? I can't see Miss Walton or Mr Hutchinson agreeing to that," said Alice.

"By moped!" said Jean-Marc triumphantly. "I'll borrow my brother's moped and meet you there."

10

Troglodytes and Shamans

The car park of the prehistoric tourist attraction was very busy and it took the coach driver several minutes to manoeuvre the large vehicle into a suitable parking place. The children filed across the road to the turnstiles. The yellow limestone cliffs towered magnificently above them.

Alice hung back as she passed through the entrance and glanced behind her several times.

"What are you looking for?" asked Sarah.

"Oh... nothing," lied Alice.

She started up the steep gravel path, still looking over her shoulder from time to time.

They walked around a gigantic model of a mammoth trapped in a pit. It was surrounded by a group of sturdy, plastic huntsmen brandishing spears. From time to time, a fake recording of the defiant animal's roars echoed hauntingly across the clearing, bringing several murmurings of "Cool!"

The teachers had booked a guided tour and a pleasant looking French lady welcomed them all in her loud, calculated English.

"This part of the site shows a reconstruction of life Paleolithic. There are hundreds of caves and rock shelters along this valley that would have been occupied by our descendants more than ten thousand years ago."

They wandered into the mouth of the first cavernous hollow, Robert mocking their tour guide with a mincing gait and pursed lips. Alice and Sarah tried not to giggle. The huge weight of the hulk of rock above them formed a jagged low ceiling not far above their heads. The guide continued her robotic narrative.

"Here we can see a reconstruction of the manufacture of clothes from reindeer skins using flint scrapers. As we move on to the next cave room, we can see a reconstruction of the interior of a family dwelling containing actual cooking pots and instruments made from wood, bone or antlers."

They drifted from one display to the next, gradually climbing to different levels of the impressive natural structure. Alice slipped to the back again.

"Pssst!"

She turned to find Jean-Marc leaning against the safety railing at the mouth of a cave. He was silhouetted against the greens, blues and purples of the valley below.

"You made it!"

"But of course! Did you think I would not?"

"No, not really. Come on. Over here."

The two conspirators slipped back through the crowds into the corner of one of the caves. The time had come to deliberately test the power of their stones.

Alice shuddered nervously.

"Are you ready?" asked Jean-Marc.

"I'm not sure. Perhaps . . ."

"Oh, come on. Maybe nothing will happen anyway! Let's do it!"

Jean-Marc held out a hand for Alice to hold. Still she hesitated.

Then at last, she made up her mind.

She took a deep breath, gripped Jean-Marc's outstretched hand and dropped her stone into his other palm, shutting her eyes tightly. Jean-Marc's fingers closed around the two cold objects.

For a few seconds, nothing happened. Alice was just about to open her eyes when she began to feel sick again. The dizziness grew and her thoughts went spinning round and round in a vortex of madness. Then, just like before, she felt herself thud onto a rough floor. She was still fiercely gripping Jean-Marc's hand and she didn't want to look. She felt icily cold.

"Mon Dieu!" cried Jean-Marc, and Alice's eyes flicked open.

They were still inside the mouth of a rock shelter high up the cliff face, but the safety barrier had gone, as had all the tourists, and driving snow was billowing in against them.

"Come on, get up!" shouted Jean-Marc. "We've got to get inside, away from this weather."

Alice followed him into the depths of the large cave where it felt a bit warmer, but she was still shivering. At one end, the roof dropped to within a few feet of the dusty floor, but they could see that there was a rough opening in the limestone at the corner. They crouched down to avoid hitting their heads on the ceiling and squeezed through the opening into a rocky passageway that took them deeper still into the cliff side. A red glow was coming from in front, along with the sounds of someone chanting in a low voice and there was a strong smell of incense.

Still stooping, they slowly approached the entrance of an inner cave. Big rocks rose up like sentinels only a few feet from the entrance. Alice looked across to the rocks, gauging the distance. She still felt giddy and sick and her eyes were stinging.

Jean-Marc gulped his breath and boldly strode across to the cover of the shadows behind the protective boulders. Crouching down, he beckoned for Alice to follow him. She took two long strides and ducked down behind him, gripping his shoulders. Cautiously, they peered over.

Right in front of them stood a bearded holy man. He wore a tunic made from skins and a necklace of animal teeth. But the most striking thing was his headdress. It was a bear's head. The enormous jaw rested on top of the man's own forehead and the rest of the fur trailed down his back enveloping him in a hairy embrace.

The smell in the cave was very strong and Alice held on to Jean-Marc's arm to steady herself against the woozy feeling in her head.

"Is that a dead body?" whispered Jean-Marc.

Alice looked past the chanting man and tried to focus her blurred eyes on the floor beneath his feet. The still body of a young woman was lying in a shallow grave encircled by stones and decorative objects. She wore one necklace made from shells and another plain choker that was threaded through a leather pouch. Red ochre had been painted on her face. She looked as if she was sleeping peacefully, but Alice knew that she was dead.

"Look!" Jean-Marc pointed suddenly at the poorly lit walls above them.

Alice began to make out primitive paintings of animals and people on horseback that almost completely covered the walls and ceiling of the entire cave. Here and there, the artist had stenciled around his own hands.

A primitive lamp made from a woven wick soaked in reindeer fat was spitting and flicking on a flat boulder that served as a table. A variety of brushes made from animal hairs bound onto sticks were strewn either side of a wooden palette. Little heaps of ground earth the colour of red ochre stood in neat lines, waiting to be mixed with more animal fat and made into paint. Roughly bound wood scaffolding loomed out of the shadows against the far wall that was the only part of the cave not yet covered with the vibrant mural.

Suddenly the holy man stopped his soothing chants. The children looked back at him and to their horror, he was looking straight at them.

"Sit here!" he commanded in a deep, soft voice. Jean-Marc and Alice froze in terror.

11

Eidor

ithout realising it, both children had understood the shaman, although his language was neither French nor English.

"I will not hurt you," the man continued. "Come, please."

He gestured for them to sit on a rough mat on the other side of the cave.

Although she was terrified, Alice felt powerless to resist. She was almost overwhelmed by the hypnotic smells and she felt herself walking around the decorative grave, almost as if she were outside of her own body. As she sat cross-legged on the matting, the man beckoned to Jean-Marc again, who cautiously circled the grave and took a seat next to Alice.

The bearded shaman lifted his gnarled club and walked over to them. He squatted down in front of them. Alice noticed that his muscular body was streaked with red paint. Behind him, the small fire crackled and billowed magenta smoke.

"I have been waiting for you," he said. Alice frowned in surprise.

"Who are you? Are you a sorcerer?" asked Jean-Marc. The man smiled.

"Not exactly," he replied. "I am Eidor the Shaman."

"Who is she... or was she?" asked Alice, pointing at the dead girl, who looked about fourteen years old.

"This is our queen. She was the ruler of this tribe. But in life she was not connected to you. Only in death. I have seen your visit in my visions and I knew that you must come when she died. It is my destiny and yours to undo the evil of others. I think you have seen some of the results of that evil?"

He looked expectantly at the children, but they stared blankly back.

"I will show you," he said.

In the dust of the cave floor Eidor drew a circle with his club. He blew across it, chanting musical, rhythmic sounds. As the two young people watched, the dust smoothed and became transparent.

The holy man moved his hand in a dance of waves and circles above the pool. Alice started to see faces growing more obvious every second, until the pool became a window into another world, like a television screen playing a bad video recording with no sound.

She recognised Lady Alys and the man seemed familiar too. In the foreground, they could see the head and shoulders of another blond-haired man with his back towards them. He wore a luxurious velvet tunic with gold braiding on the shoulders. He was spying on the other two, who were smiling at one another.

"That one looking towards us is John, isn't it?" whispered Alice. "He looks younger than I remember. What's he doing?"

"He's giving her something I think," replied Jean-Marc, as he too became absorbed in watching the scene that was playing on the ground in front of them. "It looks like the stone pendant. I don't know who the second man is, though. I can't see his face."

Eidor the Shaman suddenly steadied his hand then reversed the direction of the graceful dancing movements. The picture in the pool flickered and changed. Now they saw children dressed in rags sitting miserably on the steps of a medieval castle with begging bowls by their feet, while the crowd in front waved at a procession of knights on horseback.

"Those horses!" cried Alice. "Look at the crest on their

coats. It's the gold lions again . . . the royal crest of King Richard."

In front of the procession rode a tall, blond king.

At that moment, Eidor suddenly changed the direction of his arm movements, but still he chanted on, in his poetic rhythms. The two children waited for the fuzz to clear. This time they saw the dim interior of a vaulted chamber and they recognised the same lady immediately. But this time, tears were running down her cheeks. She rushed over to the heavy door and beat upon the thick wood. It was obviously locked or bolted from the outside. Lady Alys was being held captive.

"Look at her necklace . . . look closely! It is our stone! They WERE once joined," cried Jean-Marc wildly.

The next picture was of a row of houses in a modern street. Floodwater cascaded down the street as high as the letterboxes and a child waved frantically from an upstairs window, as if he could somehow attract their attention. Behind the houses loomed a flooded castle.

"That's Newark!" said Alice. "But it's never flooded that badly. Unless that could be . . . you don't suppose that is . . . the future, do you?" She looked at her friend. Her face was white.

Eidor changed the waving of his hand one more time. Now they were seeing flooded homes again but these were not English houses.

"That's . . ." Jean-Marc paused and looked at Alice. They both spoke together.

"Rocamadour!"

They were looking at each other in disbelief when the shaman stopped chanting.

"What does it all mean?" asked Alice.

Eidor stood up, beckoning at them to follow him. He crouched beside the girl's body and lifted the pouch that hung around her neck.

"I think you know what is in here," he said softly.

For a moment, the two youngsters looked at him in confusion.

Then Alice understood.

"The stone," she breathed.

12

Time Triggers

The shaman's eyes were almost black. They shone with an inner strength and knowledge. The stitching on the leather of his knee length tunic was exactly regular and was punctuated every few centimetres by a bear-claw that was woven into the seam and gave the effect of decorative fringing. He wore three copper rings above his left elbow, while the right arm was tattooed in red and black triangular markings. He looked magnificent in the flickering red light of the burial cave. His voice was calm and reassuring.

"You have a destiny to fulfill and you must make more journeys. The spirits have chosen you because you can feel time as it truly is. You have a gift and you can use it to bring about that which is right, if you choose wisely."

Alice raised her eyebrows slightly.

"What do you mean by *feel* time...? Sometimes I can't even tell the time properly, unless I really concentrate."

"Time can only be felt. It cannot be trapped and measured as the humans of your age try to do. Time only exists as *changes* and change is infinitely random. But those who sense time as a power can harness it. Some will turn its power into action that is right and bring about positive change, but others..."

The holy man hesitated with a pained far away look in his eyes.

"Others," he continued, "will try to use what they feel to make negative change that is not right. Such change can bring catastrophe to the earth and all the cosmos. It is your destiny, and the destiny of others like you, to deflect such actions if you can feel your way to do so. That is why you found the fragments of the cosmic stone and knew their power."

Jean-Marc and Alice exchanged excited looks.

"Why do you call it the cosmic stone?" asked Alice.

"Because it came to me from the sky one night in a ball of flame. It is a Time Trigger."

Alice's eyes widened.

"Time Triggers are objects which enable those like you, with the gift, to harness the power of time in order to alter actions that have already been. I think people of your millennium who have some knowledge have come to call these journeys time travel. Triggers can vary. This one is from the outer worlds beyond our earth. But sometimes they are stones or minerals found here, or even those that have been worked by human hands. Because you have the gift, you will know such objects when you encounter them in the future, for you will almost certainly have cause to journey many times more during your time on earth, now that you have been selected by the spirits."

"I bet it's a meteorite!" said Jean-Marc.

"Yes! Of course," said Alice. She was thoughtful.

"But what *spirits?*" she asked.

"Spirits are not of this earth. As one of the most chosen, I still can feel them only. Sometimes I almost see them when I have taken medicines that give me dreams. Those are the most sacred of moments when I come close to union with them and close to the ultimate truth. Even I do not know their true form. Humanity has many names for them. Some have felt them to be parts of the same oneness. Others feel them distinctly. We can never know until we join them in the ultimate change of death."

He looked down at the still body of the young queen and smiled.

71

"So what do those visions mean?" asked Jean-Marc, pointing over towards the circle drawn in the dust.

Eidor the Shaman did not reply. He merely smiled at them both and waited.

"Somehow, John found or took the stone when he was younger and gave it as a pendant to Lady Alys," suggested Alice.

"And Richard... he was John's brother wasn't he?" Jean-Marc looked at Alice for confirmation.

"Yes, his older brother."

"...well, Richard was also involved. It was him spying on John when he gave the necklace. I think he was jealous. Alys said herself that she was engaged to Richard and not John. So Richard imprisoned Alys in one of his castles." Jean-Marc was looking pleased with himself.

"And later, John smashed the stone when Alys wouldn't run away with him," said Alice.

Jean-Marc frowned. "And how do the floods fit in? They haven't happened yet."

"No... but they're about to! My teacher told us there's heavy rain forecast both here and in England," said Alice gravely. She looked dreamily into the air, deep in thought.

"Of course! That's how my half got into the garden... after flooding I mean." She voiced her thoughts in a cascade of excitement, hardly breathing in between. "They were freak floods, but not as bad as in your visions. The River Trent flooded away from the town centre towards where I live. It carried the stone from the castle to my garden! And... hang on! I know I've come across weird flooding in connection with Newark somewhere before. Now where was it?... I know! It's incredible! It must be connected! There were storms and floods just before King John died in Newark... I remember reading about it on the boards in the tourist centre at the castle."

"Sounds good. But we still don't know how the stone got from the queen's body in the first place, do we?" said Jean-Marc.

Still the shaman did not speak.

"I bet John or Richard took it. I bet they came here too," said Alice. Then she remembered something else.

"English kings came to Rocamadour as pilgrims!"

Alice looked at the magnificent black and red paintings of horses, deer and bulls that roamed triumphantly across the walls and ceiling of the glowing cave. In the flickering firelight they seemed almost real, as if they might jump down beside her at any moment.

"Do we have to put the stone back in your queen's pouch?" asked Jean-Marc. "If we do, will it stop those new floods happening?"

"Yes and no," said Eidor. "I think you can see what it is that you must do to restore balance." He looked pleased with them.

"You can only undo change by going back to when it occurred. You must journey to the age when the stone was originally taken and replace it. Only then can you alter the power from negative, destructive energy to bring about positive change."

Jean-Marc and Alice looked at one another. Alice was grinning at the prospect. She was beginning to enjoy this time travel business.

Just then, they heard the bellowing sound of a horn being blown from beyond the entrance to the cave.

"You must go now. Use the stone," said Eidor in his slow, commanding voice.

The scuffle of footsteps was in the outer cavern now. The horn sounded again, but this time it was much closer.

Alice saw Jean-Marc take the two stones into his hand. She felt a pang of sorrow at the thought of leaving this mysterious man who she now felt she had known for ages.

"Will we see you again?" she suddenly asked.

"One day, perhaps," he said, smiling.

Then he closed his eyes, raised his ancient club and started to chant the melodious song again.

Alice turned to Jean-Marc and he nodded. She took his hand as he tightly pressed together the two fragments of the Time Trigger meteorite. Alice glanced at the shaman one more time and saw that his shadow cast the silhouette of a bear alongside the herds of other great beasts that stampeded along the wall behind. She closed her eyes and concentrated her thoughts. Within moments her mind was once again travelling the highways of time in a glorious confusion of colour, warmth and smell.

13

𝕽umbled

𝕿 he first thing Alice noticed was that she felt warm again. She opened her eyes to a worm's eye view of the turquoise sky of a hot French summer's day. The blue canvas was interrupted by the straight black rods of the railings that protected tourists from plunging over the edge into the valley below. She stood up next to Jean-Marc. Dozens of unconcerned people milled around, looking at the reconstructions of Paleolithic life. The two adventurers had returned to the same outer cave from which they had time-travelled.

They both turned to look for the entrance to the passage in the back corner of the cave. But instead of the low doorway through which they had squeezed, there was a huge pile of gigantic ancient boulders stacked right up to the roof.

"I bet no-one knows about the beautiful burial chamber behind!" whispered Alice, feeling somehow relieved.

They grinned at each other in the knowledge of their shared secret.

"I think I should catch up with the others," said Alice, looking in the direction of the guided tour.

"We have to try and go back to when the stone was taken, don't we?" asked Jean-Marc.

"Now?" said Alice in alarm. "I think I ought to check I haven't been missed. Besides, I need to think about this a bit. I need to get my head around everything... write it down or something... and try and make some sense of it all."

"Ha!" laughed her friend. "Sense! There is no sense! The

whole thing is ridiculous really!"

Alice shot him a cross scowl.

"Don't you think it happened then?"

Jean-Marc's face became quite serious.

"Yes. I do believe that we travelled back to a cold, pre-historic time. And I know that we really were face to face with a Stone Age magic man." He hesitated. "I'm afraid, Alice. You were right when you said we were messing about with something powerful. If we take up this quest to return the stone to it's rightful resting place, it could be dangerous. We might bump into those two English princes and I don't think they'll be too friendly!"

Alice smiled at him and her eyes sparkled. Jean-Marc looked intently at her for a few seconds, before a mischievous grin crept across his sun-tanned face. For a moment, they felt a tremour of another kind of magic.

They were startled by a nearby voice calling their names and they jumped round to be greeted by Robert and Sarah running towards them.

"There you are!" shouted Sarah. Then she noticed Jean-Marc.

"Oh! I see!" she giggled.

Alice tried to look very calm and relaxed.

"What's the matter, Sair?" she asked in a flat voice.

"We've been given half an hour to look around on our own. Robert said he thought he'd seen you go back this way, so we've come to find you. That's O.K. isn't it?"

Sarah's voice was rather sarcastic with the last remark.

Alice smiled at her friend.

"Of course it is. Er... This is Jean-Marc. Jean-Marc, meet Sarah."

"Hello!" beamed Sarah. "Oh! I mean... *bonjour!*"

Jean-Marc gave Sarah the satisfaction of a gallant nod.

"Enchanté, Madamoiselle," he said, in his clearest, most polite voice.

Robert was looking at them suspiciously.

"You just happened to be here, I suppose," he said to Jean-Marc in a slightly unpleasant voice.

"Yes. I come here quite a lot, actually. I have a ... how do you call it in English? ... Ah, yes. A season ticket. I like the minerals and fossils in the shop. But I think it's time I went now. Maybe I'll see you later on?"

Sarah smiled emphatically at this suggestion, but Robert was not going to be fooled.

"You've used those stones, haven't you!" he hissed in Alice's ear.

She took a step away from him and brushed against Jean-Marc. As she did so, Alice felt him put a familiar cold object into her hand.

"We've been studying the burial rites of the Paleolithic peoples," she said. "Jean-Marc was explaining it to me. I'm going to use it in my project."

"That sounds a bit grim!" said Sarah.

Robert scoffed.

Jean-Marc gave the others a wave and started to walk back along the path, excusing himself to the many tourists he bumped into as he hurried down.

"We WILL see you later!" Robert yelled after him. He turned to Alice, who was fumbling with her clipboard and starting to make impressive diagrams and notes for her project.

"I want to go with you, too. You know what I mean!" he said, glaring. The true meaning of his request was lost on Sarah, but Alice knew all too well what he meant. She smiled a big smile at Robert, and said nothing.

"Can I come too?" asked Sarah hopefully.

"I don't see why not," said Alice, still looking at Robert. He stomped off towards the next cave display.

"He's jealous!" giggled Sarah.

14

Hair Braids and Langoustines

Alice's project was coming on very nicely now. She made pencil sketches of Paleolithic tools and pots to add a personal touch, and bought four postcards to use as illustrations. The free tourist leaflet in the gift shop looked a promising source of colourful material that she could stick into her folder too. They were allowed to choose almost any aspect of the French trip on which to produce a project, as long as the teachers approved. Miss Walton looked most impressed by Alice's idea to compare Stone Age and medieval troglodyte rituals. Robert and Luke's new idea about wine making was less favorably received, but somehow the boys managed to persuade her that it would have some educational value.

The next part of the boy's work was apparently going to need research in the supermarket in Montignac on the way home, where they were stopping off to buy souvenirs and presents.

It was early evening. Back home in England the shops would have been preparing to close for the night, but in France, the little town was coming to life for the evening rush. The locals were emerging and heading for the *boulangerie* to buy a fresh *baguette* for supper. There were plenty of bicycles and a lot of impatient honking from the battalions of battered old Renaults and Peugeots being driven into town from the surrounding farms.

The roadside tables at the numerous cafes and *tabacs* along the riverfront were packed with tourists and locals alike, all enjoying a leisurely drink in the warm evening sunshine. A group of sunburnt Frenchmen sat on a bench under the shade of an olive tree and were commentating earnestly on the developments of the *boules* match being played on the dusty town square.

To the children's delight, tonight was the night for the weekly evening market and the town centre was dotted with brightly coloured stalls selling a tantalizing variety of goods.

The coach driver parked in a shady car park on the shore of the river and the children tumbled off excitedly.

"Where shall we go first?" asked Sarah.

"Oh, the market, definitely!" said Alice. "Come on! Let's see what there is!"

The two girls skipped off impatiently.

"Hey, Sair! Hair braids!" said Alice suddenly, noticing the display of coloured threads on the wall behind a jewellery stall. "I had one of those put in two years ago. Do you remember?"

"Yes, I do. It was cool! You had to hide it in a plait for school. Do you fancy another one?" Sarah chuckled mischievously.

The young stallholder was called Marie and she came from Bordeaux, where she was a student. She was earning money during the holidays like many students, by travelling with the country markets all over the south of France. She started to wind silk threads into blocks of bright colour in Alice's hair.

"I've braided the hair of so many English girls this summer. Can you not have it done in England?" she asked.

"I've looked, but I can't find anywhere near where we live that does this," said Alice. "I've tried with a kit my mum bought me, but the braid kept falling out!"

They all laughed. It wasn't long before Alice's braid was finished and it was Sarah's turn.

Someone poked Alice in her back.

"Hey!" She swung round to meet Robert who was wielding an African drum made of real animal hide stretched over the carved barrel. He tapped it rhythmically and it gave a clear musical sound.

"What do you think?" he grinned at Alice.

"It's... Well, I suppose it's..."

"Cool?" Robert helped her.

"Yes, it's great. It looks very expensive."

"I bartered for it," announced Robert triumphantly. "The man wanted three times as much originally ... thirty euros, but I said I didn't have much money left. I offered him ten. At first he said it wasn't enough, so we looked disappointed and started to walk away. But he came after us and agreed to my price! He brought the drum all the way from Africa you know!"

"It wasn't really the last of his money!" added Luke, looking impressed at his friend's conquest.

Robert was watching the young woman's deft hands as she put the finishing touches to Sarah's braid.

"Would your boyfriend like a braid?" she asked Alice in French. Alice blushed slightly and laughed. She translated the request, leaving out the reference to boyfriend.

"Er... no thanks!" said Robert, trying to be polite. *"Non, merci."*

"What a shame!" said Marie the French woman, "I think a black and gold one would look good in all that blond English hair!"

The girls paid Marie for the braids.

"Thanks!" she said. "Make the most of the sunshine tonight. I hear there's a big storm on the way."

Alice suddenly remembered the shaman's visions of terrible flooding. She felt for her stone in the bottom of her shorts pocket and wondered whether they should head back to the coach.

"What's the matter, Alice?" asked Robert.

"Oh ... I'm not sure. How long did we have here?"

"Oh, we've got another half hour yet," said Luke. "Let's go to the supermarket!"

Alice nodded agreement, trying to hide her reluctance. She now wanted to get back and find a way to meet Jean-Marc. They all crossed the road and walked along to the large *Intermarché*. The boys went off to look in the wine section for some ideas towards their project, leaving Alice and Sarah to wander up and down the aisles. Sarah took a hand basket and helped herself to several bars of French chocolate. The sweets distracted Alice too, and she took some interesting looking *Haribos* for her little sister and some strong dark chocolate in thin bars that she knew her grandad would like.

"Urrgh! Look at these, Alice!" called Sarah. She had found the fish counter and was looking at the tank of live crabs and lobsters. "Cor! They stink! I thought lobsters were orange, not that boring, dull blue colour?"

"They'll turn orange when they're boiled," said Alice, who had often watched in disgust, as either her mother or her aunt put the wretched creatures into pans of boiling water.

"Oh, no! Those big shrimpy things are still moving ... and that man's having a whole bag of them!"

Sure enough, a Frenchman was buying a large bag of very fresh *langoustines*. Their shells were almost translucent. The girls watched in horror as he put the gyrating plastic sac into his trolley.

"Yuk! Disgusting!" agreed Alice. Despite her frequent trips to France she had never become accustomed to buying live seafood for supper.

After investigating the lovely smells of the fresh bread at the next counter, and admiring the display of raspberry and apple tarts, the girls paid for their purchases at the checkout and sat down on a bench outside to wait for the boys. They raised their faces towards the sun and Alice closed her eyes. She felt in her pocket for the stone and let her hand close around it. It still felt cold.

She thought about Jean-Marc. How could she escape the watchful eyes of her teachers to meet him? Was it really their destiny to travel back in time and replace the stone? And then there was Robert. What was she going to do about him? It was true that he had been her accomplice on her first journey. Did that mean he also possessed the powers to use Time Triggers? But he hadn't found one. Until this trip she was starting to quite like him, but recently, he'd become selfish. Could the stones somehow make some people evil or something?

She thought back to how Prince John had behaved. What was it he'd said?

"May the shaman's curse be on you," she murmured.

An idea was forming in her mind, but she couldn't quite make sense of it all yet. Something was missing. Oh! It was all so difficult!

15

Storm

A lice climbed off the coach at *La Grange aux Fleurs* and walked past some of the other girls. She tried a smile at Tessa. To her surprise, Tessa detached herself from the rest and smiled back.

"I really like your hair braid, Alice," she said.

"Oh! Thanks! What did you buy in the market?"

"This..." Tessa produced a floppy lizard. Its body was made from sparkly green material and stuffed with sand. "It's a ghekko!"

"Oh! It's lovely. May I hold it?"

Alice wondered why she was suddenly in favour. The two other girls that usually hung around Tessa were looking sheepishly in her direction. They looked lost without their leader.

"Help yourself," Tessa beamed with big-headed satisfaction, as Alice admired the prize buy. "You are lucky to speak French so well. I wish I had French cousins."

Sarah bounded up.

"Nice lizard!" she said, not quite sure what to make of the interaction between her friend and the other girl.

Tessa reached out and took her trophy back with a courteous smile. Then she turned back to her gang and led them off down the track towards the camp barns.

"What was all that about?" asked Sarah uneasily.

"I don't know. She was admiring my braid and my French. Amazing, really!"

"She's after something. Watch it, Alice!"

"Maybe she just wanted to be friendly. It must be hard being bitchy all the time!"

Alice wanted to be charitable. Perhaps the bully was

beginning to tire of the battle, but Alice would never really trust the self appointed class queen.

She was beginning to feel really hungry.

"I'm starving! Someone said we're having a barbeque for tea. Come on!"

Sure enough, the fantastic aroma of chargrilled sausages and steak wafted down to meet them.

Everyone spent the evening swimming, eating and sunbathing. Even the two teachers looked as if they were having a good time, despite a few clearly audible taunts about the sight of Mr Hutchinson in swimming trunks. Miss Walton remained fully clothed in her blouse and skirt, and assumed a dignified repose with a thick historical novel at the side of the pool.

The young people laughed and joked until the sun finally descended behind the distant hills amid the nocturnal chorus of the cicadas. The tired children sloped off to their bunks one by one.

As Alice lay uncomfortably on the sausage shaped pillow, she drifted off to sleep feeling slightly guilty that she'd forgotten all about her stone and it's awesome power. She was not asleep for long.

A violent crash shattered the night stillness. Alice's eyes opened immediately. She waited nervously, with her senses straining in the darkness. A moment later, the little room was brilliantly illuminated through a gap in the curtains by a fleeting, silent pulse of brightest white. Alice clapped her hands over her ears and started to count. She only got to three, when a second mighty crack pierced the silence.

"Are you awake?" came a tiny whisper from the bunk below.

"Of course I am!"

One of the girls opposite sat up.

Another white flash lit up the sky and the girls counted aloud together.

"One... two... "

The terrifying roll rumbled through the barn and the window shook. Alice wasn't sure whether she was excited or scared. She thought of home, with her mum asleep in the next room.

One crack followed another relentlessly and the night was alight with the blinding display.

Then the rain came. It started slowly with a gentle pattering against the window, but quickly deteriorated into hostile torrents that smote the barns with cruel determination. Water started to leak under the bottom of the door and through one side of the window frame.

Alice jumped down and peeped through the gap in the curtains.

The silhouetted trees bent alarmingly low in the violent winds and there was an awful lot of water on the ground already. Puddles grew into lakes and then joined up to run down the slope of the drive in rivers. Sheets of rain pelted the buildings in a brilliantly lit dance to the irregular rhythm of the thunderous percussion.

Alice was captivated.

Then she remembered.

"The floods!"

"Alice, please come away from the window!" urged Sarah.

Alice closed the curtains and turned back towards her bed. She was deep in thought. She had to get to Jean-Marc somehow. But it was impossible right now. She huddled under her duvet and watched the lightning pierce every tiny chink around the curtains. She would have to wait until morning.

The storm raged for over an hour and the other three girls tried to boost each other's morale by playing animal, vegetable, mineral. Alice said she was too tired too join in. Her mind reeled with getaway plans and replacing the stone.

She found herself being woken up in daylight by Miss Walton's voice.

"Good morning girls! You've overslept. We've had to cancel our planned visit to the walled town of Domme, I'm afraid." The girls sat up one by one. "No doubt you heard the storm last night. Apparently there's been a lot of damage on the roads . . . fallen trees and cables, and a lot of minor flooding. And the rain looks set to continue for the time being. So we're going to have a day in camp. But there's lots to do, so come on now! Some of the others had breakfast an hour ago."

Miss Walton breezed off, and the girls could hear a muffled encore of their wake up lecture being delivered next door.

"Urghhh!" Sarah fell back onto her pillow and pulled her duvet over her head.

Alice's eyes were stinging from lack of sleep and her head ached. But as she lay there getting the last few minutes of warmth and comfort, she afforded herself a smile. It must be possible to sneak off to find Jean-Marc now.

But she was wrong.

The rain continued all morning and the children were confined to the big eating barn after breakfast, to design posters for an impromptu competition organised by Mr Hutchinson. Alice was feeling increasingly frustrated. There just never seemed to be an opportunity to excuse herself.

"Come on Alice!" encouraged Sarah. "You're usually the artistic one. What else can we add? It was your idea after all."

She was staring at their poster for a medieval jousting competition. Alice tried to concentrate on the task. Sarah's drawing of a knight on horseback was not great.

86

Alice took her rubber and rubbed out his top half. She started sketching the different tones of a suit of armour, complete with a tall helmet that obscured all but his eyes.

"This way, we don't need to worry about getting his face right!" she joked.

Alice reached for her gel pens and almost absent-mindedly, she created a bright red drape over the hind-quarters of the horse with three gold lions on.

"Wow! That's great!" said Sarah.

From the table behind, Robert turned to look at the girls' work. Alice waited for his response. When he saw the coat of arms he looked up at Alice with a quizzical expression. Then he smiled.

"Nice drawing," he said.

They looked at each other intently for a few seconds.

Madame Magret appeared through the doors carrying a tray of homemade vanilla biscuits. Her husband followed with a crate of cola and hauled it onto the serving table at the front of the barn. It was time for a break. The moreish biscuit was some consolation for Alice's frustration.

"You did go back again... in the cave, didn't you?" said Robert quietly, sitting down in the place next to Alice.

She looked at him as she took another bite of her cookie. His eyes were friendly now. She could see no trace of the momentary madness he had showed the other day in the dining hall of the medieval castle. Could she trust him? She badly needed to confide in someone.

"Yes," she replied simply.

Robert watched her, waiting for her next move.

"We went much further back, Rob. We went back to the Stone Age."

16

𝕬 𝕽endezvous 𝕬greed

Robert's eyes widened as Alice recounted the extraordinary visit to the burial cave of the Paleolithic troglodytes and the encounter with Eidor the Shaman.

"Do you think I am a time traveller too?" asked Robert hopefully.

"Possibly..." Alice didn't want to hurt his feelings. "Well... it could have been because you were touching me..." She saw a flutter of sadness in his eyes. "...maybe you just haven't found your first Trigger yet!"

"How are you going to get to Jean-Marc then?" asked Robert. He sounded as if he was trying to change the subject.

Alice sighed.

"I really don't know. I've been trying to work that one out all morning!"

"We... I mean you, do need to go back."

They were thoughtful for a few moments.

"Alice,"

"Yes."

"Can I come too?"

Alice studied Robert's blond features. He looked so nice now. Suddenly, she hoped she wasn't blushing.

"I suppose so. But maybe we should ask Jean-Marc."

Robert's face melted into a frown.

"Why do I think he's not gonna like that idea?"

"I'll speak to him. You know about everything now anyway. And maybe we'll need as many of us as possible. I've got a nasty feeling that we might come face to face with Prince John and King Richard."

Robert grinned. "Actually, that sounds quite good!"

"Oh, don't be an idiot! They don't look very friendly, especially Richard. They could probably kill us!"

"Maybe. Maybe not. Anyway... they shouldn't be able to see us, should they?"

"I wouldn't be so sure. Eidor could."

Miss Walton loomed in front of them.

"Your aunt has telephoned, Alice. From Montignac. She asked if she could drive over and collect you this evening, as long as the roads are clear. I said yes. Is that O.K. with you?"

"Oh! Yes. That's great. Thanks! Oh... but when am I coming back?"

"Tomorrow evening," replied her teacher. "Don't you want to go?"

"Oh! Yes... of course!" Alice tried to look very enthusiastic again. Then suddenly she had an idea. "Miss Walton... would it be O.K. if I go down to the farm to ask Jean-Marc Magret something? It's just that he thought he knew one of my cousins and he had some photos or something he wanted me to take to them... Robert could come too?"

"Umm. Yes. I suppose so. Be back as soon as you can though. You've both got quite a lot of work to do on those projects I think!"

With that, Miss Walton minced off to inspect the offerings of the other students. Robert winked at Alice.

They set off down the drive sharing an umbrella.

When they got to the front of the old farmhouse, Alice bounded up the stone steps.

"Excusez moi, Madame," she said, when Madame Magret finally answered. In her best French, Alice asked if they could speak to Jean-Marc. His mother told them he was in his den and she was sure he would be pleased to see them if they would like to go and find him. Alice thanked her and led a nervous looking Robert into the

open fronted barn next-door and called up to Jean-Marc.

The familiar dark hair of the French boy popped over the edge of the platform and he grinned down. The grin vanished when he saw Robert.

"What's HE doing here?"

"It's O.K. Jean-Marc. I told him everything." Alice climbed the ladder. "Maybe I shouldn't have... but I did. O.K? He's been very understanding. I don't think he meant to be rude before. Can't you two be friends?"

Jean-Marc grunted disbelievingly.

"Please, Jean-Marc!" pleaded Alice. "We might need him."

Reluctantly, the French boy retreated from the top of the ladder. It was a sign that they could both go up.

Robert sat down on the old armchair.

"Sorry... about the other day," he mumbled. "I promise I'll be fine next time..."

"Huh!" Jean-Marc fiddled with a jar of coloured sands on one of the bookshelves.

There was an awkward silence.

"How are we going to get back to the cave, then?" said Jean-Marc eventually.

"I think I know how," said Alice. "My Aunt is coming to collect me tonight. I'll be at her house tomorrow. I think I could persuade her to take me back to the troglodyte city for my research or something. Could you meet me there?"

"But of course! On my brother's moped..." he paused to look at Robert.

"Please... I could get away somehow. We're still gonna be in the camp all day tomorrow I think. Couldn't I come on the bike too?"

"Surely he could, Jean-Marc?" said Alice.

"Maybe."

"Shall we say twelve midday?" continued Alice. "I

could ring you from my aunt's house if something goes wrong."

"Sounds good to me." Jean-Marc looked sternly at Robert. "Be here at eleven. I won't wait if you're late."

17

Numero Cinq, Rue Bonnac

The rain didn't ease at all. It was still falling heavily when the wheels of an old *Renault Clio* crunched to a standstill on the shiny gravel drive at five o'clock that afternoon. The driver was a frizzy-haired lady wearing an orange T-shirt, suede boots and baggy, printed cotton trousers. Alice was ready. She rushed over and gave her aunt an enormous hug. Aunt Bonnie kissed her niece fondly before exchanging pleasantries with Miss Walton and Mr Hutchinson.

"Time to chill with your laid-back cousins, eh?" Aunt Bonnie laughed, as they drove off.

Alice listened contentedly to the ramblings of her favourite aunt. Bonnie had a new boyfriend. "He's an artist, you know. Oils mostly. Impressionist landscapes *à la* Monet. At last I've found a soul mate Alice!"

They soon arrived at the familiar, old façade of *numero cinq, Rue Bonnac*. In fact, the house looked so old and scruffy that from the front, Alice though it looked uninhabited. But like so many French home-owners, her aunt did not concern herself with repairing cracked plaster. They entered the house through the *sous-sol,* which was chock-a-block with washing, sun-lounger mattresses and bicycles. As they climbed the stairs and entered the kitchen, Alice smelt a wonderful aroma of garlic and fresh bread.

"Alice!"

She was greeted with kisses from her cousins, Helen and Chloe, and they introduced her to Philippe, Aunt Bonnie's new partner. Several other family friends arrived and wine was opened and olives offered round, before everyone took their places at the table.

As the meal went on, and cheeses were followed by rich chocolate pudding, and the grown-ups seemed to be getting very merry indeed, Alice wondered how she was going to get around to proposing a trip to the troglodyte cave.

Her chance came when Aunt Bonnie disappeared off in search of more wine. Alice followed her into the kitchen.

"Bonnie," she began.

"What is it, *ma petite?*"

"I have a small problem about tomorrow, and I was hoping you might be able to help me..."

Alice briefly explained her need to re-visit the prehistoric caves in order to complete some project work.

"Of course, you can go! If I can't run you over, I'm sure Philippe, or one of the others will be free."

Bonnie winked at Alice, before popping the cork from the bottle of wine and sweeping back to her guests.

Alice relaxed and spent the rest of the evening with her cousins, messing about with their stereos. Her bedroom was bright and airy, with straw coloured hessian covering the walls and a faint aroma of roses, from the bowl of tiny dried rosebuds on the dressing table. She slept well, lulled by the constant pattering of the rain against the shuttered window.

She awoke to the familiar smell of a steaming mug of English tea.

"What time did you say you'd like to be at the caves?" said her aunt, as she opened the window just long enough to fold back the maroon shutters against the outside wall, before closing the glass to keep out the rain.

"Um... about twelve," said Alice sleepily.

"Aha. Well . . . it's quarter past eleven now, so . . ."

"What! Oh, no!" exclaimed Alice in dismay as she leapt out of bed.

Then she remembered she was relying on her aunt for a lift to the caves.

"Um . . . will you be able to . . ."

"Don't worry! My car, humble though it is, is at your disposal as soon as you're dressed."

Aunt Bonnie was smiling at her niece.

"Oh, your cousins asked if they could go with you, but I got the feeling that you might want to be alone, or at least free from *uninvited* company for a little while? So I suggested they might like to accompany Philippe to the art market this morning, which they've been asking to do for ages. Did I guess right?"

Bonnie raised one eyebrow in a quizzical grin.

Alice felt herself blushing slightly. Aunt Bonnie was so cool. She gave her a big hug. Pity about the art market, though. It sounded good.

"Thank you." It was all she could think of to say.

"Jolly good. Right. When you're ready. Will an hour there be long enough?"

"Oh, yes! Loads of time. Thanks Bonnie. You're a star!"

"It's raining really heavily back in England, you know," said Bonnie, tidying the duvet. "The rivers are flooding all over the place, just like here. The army has been called in to rescue stranded people by boat, and even helicopter."

"What about the River Trent . . . in Newark?" said Alice in alarm.

"Your Mum e-mailed to say that all's well at home, up to now anyway. But she did say it's going to be touch and go if this rain doesn't stop soon. Newark Castle could be badly damaged by the floodwaters, apparently. Now then, come on! Chop! Chop! You've got a deadline, re-member!"

A gentle draft blew through the window and brushed Alice's cheeks. She sensed a restless, powerful energy.

"I think the floods will go down ... if only we can put the Time Trigger back in its rightful place," she murmured to herself.

More than ever, she needed to get to the others and try to replace the stone.

18

The Plantagenet Princes

Alice dressed quickly and set off with her aunt in the old Renault. Before long, she found herself standing in the shelter of the gift shop doorway at the entrance to the troglodyte caves.

It was ten past twelve, and there was still no sign of the boys. The clouds were blacker than ever and water was beginning to seep into Alice's trainers. She wished her mobile phone worked in France so she could ring Jean-Marc and find out where they were.

Alice looked through the shop window for the umpteenth time and played at choosing which top ten fossils she would pick, if she had the money to buy them all. The stern lady behind the counter looked back at her and Alice shifted her feet uncomfortably.

She was just beginning to wonder whether to go on alone when she heard the familiar chugging of a moped and saw Jean-Marc waving at her. Robert slowly unstuck himself from the back of the bike. Rain was dripping down his neck and he shook his mop of soaking hair, spraying droplets of water everywhere. Alice couldn't help but giggle.

"You look like my neighbour's dog after a swim in the river!" she shouted.

Jean-Marc locked up his brother's moped and started up the slope to Alice.

"Sorry! I could hardly see through all this rain. I had to slow down a bit, and there was a hold up on the main road near Rocamadour ... flooding I think."

Alice noted with satisfaction that the two boys seemed to be getting on better.

They paid for their tickets and walked up the path to the caves. It was a relief to get out of the rain, but the sky was now so dark that it was quite difficult to see the displays and models.

They stopped close to the spot where Alice and Jean-Marc had travelled the last time. Alice gently brought out her half of the stone and cradled it in her palm. Jean-Marc did the same and they stared nervously at the Time Trigger.

"Who's gonna hold them?" said Robert eventually.

"Are we sure about this?" murmured Jean-Marc. His usually tanned face had gone quite pale. "Suppose we end up ... well ... anywhere!"

"We won't," said Alice. She reached out and plopped her half in Jean-Marc's hand and linked arms with him. Robert took her other hand.

Jean-Marc slowly closed his hand over the stones and pressed them together. Within seconds, they were all spinning in a whirl of bright colour.

Alice concentrated her thoughts on the vision of the two young princes she had seen in the shaman's cave. She felt warm, velvety rushes of air that melted suddenly into a deep, dry coldness making her gasp. Her knees grazed against a rough floor. The pain made her wince but she couldn't afford to dwell on her injuries. They had travelled again.

"Where are we? What time is this?" said Robert.

There were signs that the caves were being lived in. A corbelled balcony had been fitted around the edge of the cliff face, giving the only access to the caves beyond. Under siege, this fantastic dwelling would be an impregnable fortress. At one place higher up, the whole of the front of the caves was now covered in medieval wooden house fronts, complete with beamed roofs and windows. That level was accessed via a footbridge across a wide chasm that would otherwise have cut off the inhabitants completely. There was a strong smell of wood burning fires. Lamps, dried food and cross bows were hanging from the cave ceiling above their heads, and a rusty shield was propped against the wall next to a heavy, medieval sword.

"Get down!" shouted Robert suddenly.

They could hear someone running towards them across the footbridge. Jean-Marc looked round for somewhere to hide, but it was too late. A young man ran into the cave straight in front of them. His shoulder length brown hair was curled at the bottom and beneath his trailing, fur-lined mantle, he wore a woollen tunic and hose, with short leather boots. The white of a linen undershirt glinted around his neck as he panted rapidly. But just like before, he did not see the three visitors from a later age. He looked as if he was himself searching for somewhere to hide.

"It's John!" whispered Alice in amazement.

Jean-Marc and Robert nodded.

The young prince noticed a boulder in one corner and to his obvious pleasure, it concealed the entrance to a passageway. He ducked inside.

Before the other three could follow, a second slightly older youth ran into the cave, holding a flaming torch. He wore a similar woollen, belted tunic, thick hose and short boots. But he also wore a bright red, silky over-tunic, and his hooded cloak was lined with luxurious grey-blue and white pelts. His thick, blond hair was more elaborately curled.

"O.K. I know you're in here somewhere! I'll get you! You can't hide from me, little brother!" he sneered. He spoke in French, but even Robert understood.

The other three looked at each other. No-one said anything, but they all knew they were standing only a few metres from the young man who would one day be King Richard the Lionheart.

Richard spied the entrance to the passageway and with a yelp of pleasure he too squeezed through and disappeared from view.

"Why did he speak in French? I thought he was King of England," said Jean-Marc.

"Because he was born in France," said Alice. "His mother was French... Eleanor of Aquitaine... I remember reading it on that computer stuff you found."

"Oh, yeah."

"We have to follow them, don't we?" said Robert.

"Yep! Come on, then!" said Alice.

"Hang on!" called Jean-Marc. "Let's get a plan. What exactly are we going to try and do?"

Robert looked momentarily confused.

"Well, I thought the plan was to put back the stone, wasn't it?"

"Yes. But I don't think they've even taken it yet. I think we'll have to be very careful. I don't feel very good about all this."

"Come on, Jean-Marc. We've come this far. I think we have to go and see what's happening at least. We have to try," said Alice.

"I suppose so. But don't do anything without discussing it first, Robert."

Robert shrugged his shoulders. As they got to the boulder, Jean-Marc pushed to the front and they edged down the low, dark passage. Ahead of them, amber light danced and flickered. Alice's heart was pounding fast.

They reached the entrance to the cave beyond. Sure enough, it was the ancient burial chamber where Alice and Jean-Marc had met Eidor the Shaman. But this time, there were no pleasant incense smells and the only light was from Richard's flare. It was dry, dusty and cold.

John was backed into the far corner, crouching on the rocks that had once been a table for art materials. Alice looked up at the walls of the cave. She could just make out some of the dancing animal forms that decorated the hidden chamber.

Richard was taunting John with the flare.

"Told you I'd catch you! What are you going to pay me to release you then?" he laughed.

"I haven't got much left! What are you going to do to me anyway? You can't stand there for ever!"

"I could roll that stone over the entrance to this cave and leave you here to rot! After all, we've sneaked across into French territory. Father has no royal privileges hereabouts. I doubt even Mother could get you freed if I send word that there's an English spy holed up among these French cave-dwelling ruffians! And how would darling little Alys manage then, eh? She'd come running to me and beg me to tell where you are . . . and then I'd make her tell me she loved me, and only me, otherwise I wouldn't save you! Ha!"

"You evil coward, Richard! She'd never tell you that, even if you force her to marry you!"

"I think she will, my puny little mistake of a brother!"

"Never! And besides, you couldn't push that rock by yourself. Even you are not that strong!"

"Ha! We'll see!"

Richard started to back away towards the chamber entrance.

19

Thieves and Curses

John pointed to something on the shadowy floor. "What's that you're about to stand on?"

Richard didn't look.

"Trying to distract me, are you?"

"No. Stop, Richard! Look! There, on the floor... it's a skeleton!"

At that, Richard looked down. He jumped to one side in surprise.

"Urgh! You're right!"

John leapt down from the rock. The gruesome discovery made the brothers forget their feuding.

The eyes of their three watchers were also drawn to the find.

"It's the ancient queen!" whispered Jean-Marc.

The two princes knelt down alongside the skeleton. Richard started pushing the dirt away and prodding at the foot bones. At the other end of the skeleton, John tugged at something. The something gave way and he fell backwards, clutching his trophy. On his knees, he tried to see what had come out of the worn leather pouch.

"Jewellery!" he breathed.

Richard looked up.

"What have you got there?"

"I'm not sure. I think it must be a charm or something."

John turned protectively away from the advancing Richard.

"It's mine! I found it!"

"Yes, but let me see!"

Just then, everybody looked in the direction of the doorway, as the sound of someone scuffling along the low passageway got louder and louder.

The two princes stood up. Alice, Robert and Jean-Marc could see a glow of light getting steadily brighter until it exploded through the doorway enveloping a tall, bearded figure. He was dressed in full-length robes and cloak. In one hand he carried a flaming lantern, and in the other he had a large staff.

"Eidor?" gasped Alice.

In that moment everything changed.

John and Richard jumped back in surprise as the three children suddenly became visible. For the first time, someone of another age other than Eidor, could now see the time travellers.

Richard drew a hidden sword from under his long cloak. It made a crisp, metallic sound as the sharp edge grazed against its scabbard.

"Where in God's name did you three come from?" he cried, threatening them with the tip of the blade.

"Woah! Steady on!" breathed Robert, as he and Jean-Marc retreated with their backs against the wall.

Alice was looking at the bearded newcomer. Although his face was different and he was a much younger man, there was something familiar in his eyes.

"You are Eidor, aren't you?" she asked again.

The bearded man raised his staff. Richard's eyes flicked rapidly between his adversaries, his sword still raised. The man addressed Alice with a mysterious smile.

"No. My name is not Eidor. But the one of whom you speak, he is known to me."

"Then who are you?" said Alice.

"I am Kuy the Seer."

"The Minstrel Seer of Aquitaine?" asked Prince John.

"I am a seer to all who would know, and a minstrel to many."

"Know what?" It was Jean-Marc who spoke, from behind the point of Richard's blade.

"There is no end to what can be known. You young ones who have the power to journey through the changes of time should understand that."

Jean-Marc screwed up his face in confusion, but the seer turned to Prince John.

"The stone feels good, doesn't it? It fills you with a warming power. But it belongs here, and should remain here where it was intended. If you remove it willfully, you will be cursed. You will create much suffering for others and you will yourselves be doomed. You cannot control it."

"It's just a stone," said John, looking down at the plain rock he held in his palm.

"If you cross the spirits and play with powers too great for you to master, you will be cursed. And if it should ever be damaged in any way... it will certainly bring early death to all who have tried to possess it," warned the seer.

Richard suddenly grew tired of the attention this man was commanding.

"Oh, get out of here, before I kill you! Your talk of curses does not scare me!"

He took a ballestra-step and lunged at the holy man.

"No!" shouted Alice.

Her interruption distracted Richard and Kuy the Seer vanished back down the passageway.

Richard turned on the three time travellers.

"Why are you dressed in those strange robes? Are you minstrels or travelling poets? Or ... yes, of course! You are followers of the infidel!"

"What infidel?" said Robert, stepping forward.

"Ha! Do you jest? Only Saladin's spies would mock in

this fashion! And this one tries to confuse us by speaking in English! That jewel must be their quarry, John."

Robert replied bravely.

"No! You must not take it. The seer speaks the truth ... "

"Silence, infidel! You will come with us! Take the stone, John."

Richard advanced towards the children until the tip of his sword rested on Robert's chest. Robert glared fiercely into the eyes of his attacker.

With a flick of the sword, Richard indicated for them to move towards the passageway and Jean-Marc began to edge around the cave wall. For one minute, it seemed as if Robert might risk the sharpness of Richard's sword, as he lingered without movement. Then, reluctantly, he jerked after Jean-Marc, pushing the prince's sword from his chest with the side of his arm.

Prince John grabbed Alice and held her in front of him in an arm lock.

"Ow! You're hurting me!"

Jean-Marc looked back towards her, but was halted by the point of Richard's sword.

"Out!" shouted the prince.

Jean-Marc and Robert had no choice but to head down the passageway in front of Richard. John followed, pushing Alice roughly in front of him.

As they emerged into the outer cave, everything happened very quickly.

Robert spotted the old sword and shield propped up against the wall. He nodded almost invisibly at Jean-Marc, who followed the direction of Robert's glance.

At the mouth of the cave, Kuy the Seer raised his staff and banged it on the ground drawing Richard's attention. Robert did not hesitate. He grabbed the sword and Jean-Marc scooped up the shield. They turned to face their enemy.

At once, Richard engaged Robert's weapon, sniggering at the younger boy's frightened expression. The prince disengaged and beat against the other side of Robert's heavy blade, almost disarming him.

Again, Kuy the Seer banged his staff. This time, he pointed it at Richard, just as he was about to drive his sword at Robert. The seer chanted loudly and Richard clutched his chest, grimacing in momentary pain. He turned to look at the bearded silhouette.

"Aargh! What magic was that?"

It was enough to save Robert. He took two steps back and regained control of the mighty sword in both his hands. Alongside him, Jean-Marc lifted the shield protectively.

"Aha!" said Richard, still rubbing his chest. "I see that Saladin does train his spies in the art of combat! Excellent sport, wouldn't you say, little brother?"

At that moment, Alice kicked backwards, striking her captor's shins and twisted out of her arm lock to face him. Richard laughed.

"What's the matter, John? Always the ladies man, eh?"

"Be careful, Alice!" shouted Jean-Marc.

At the mention of her name, both princes looked at her. "Alys?" said John.

For a moment, Alice thought he almost smiled at her.

The confusion was what Robert was waiting for. In a flash, he raised his arms and bravely struck the blade of his attacker then leapt towards Alice. Jean-Marc stepped after him, but not in time to avoid the force of a cutting blow from Richard, which landed heavily on the back of the shield, sending it spinning from Jean-Marc's hand. He stumbled, cutting his cheek against the wall of the cave. As Richard raised his sword again to strike a lethal blow, Jean-Marc flung himself towards Robert.

"The stones! I'm holding the stones!" he yelled at the other two.

20

𝕳ot 𝕮hocolate

𝕬lice grabbed one of Robert's arms just as Jean-Marc reached out for the other. Not a moment too soon, they felt themselves falling through rapid swirls of time and they collapsed in a heap in the pouring rain.

Alice looked round for the others. Jean-Marc's face was grazed and bleeding and Robert was still clutching the medieval sword. He ran his hand along the back of the slightly rusty blade and smiled.

Jean-Marc grinned and nodded at him.

"You were cool, Rob," he said.

"You weren't bad yourself. Your cheek is dripping blood you know."

Jean-Marc felt in his pocket for a handkerchief. As he did so, he pulled out the two halves of the Time Trigger stone.

"Oh dear. We didn't do what we set out to, did we?"

"We'll have to go back," said Alice, gazing at the fragments of meteorite with a worried frown.

"Yep!" said Robert. "And what am I going to do with this sword then?"

"I suppose you'll have to keep it for now. I don't see what else you can do." Alice sighed wearily. "I don't fancy going back straight away though, do you?"

Jean-Marc shook his head.

"Any one hungry? There's a café I know back in Rocamadour that does great chocolate cake. I reckon we could all just squeeze onto the bike."

"Sounds great!" said Alice.

It was a very snug fit on the moped. Robert had to sit

right at the back to hold the sword without it cutting anyone. Alice was squashed between the two boys and Robert had to hold her tightly to stop himself from falling off. She consoled herself that at least being in the middle gave her the best protection against the relentless rain. They sped back down the bendy road along the river valley to Rocamadour. The river was very full now.

Jean-Marc finally stopped at the foot of the sheer cliff and wheeled the moped through the arched city gate. Alice gazed up once more at the historic city.

"Oh, no!" she suddenly exclaimed. "My aunt! She was going to collect me at one o'clock. What time is it now?"

Jean-Marc glanced at his watch.

"It's only twenty-five past twelve. It's odd, and I noticed it last time, but we don't seem to lose any time when we travel. Just as well! I'm not sure we've got time for a hot chocolate... unless you ring her on my mobile. Maybe she could come at half-past one?"

"You're a star!" said Alice. She just hoped her aunt would still be at home. Luckily, she was.

"Done!" pronounced Alice, as she returned the phone to Jean-Marc. "Where's that café then?"

Jean-Marc led them along the narrow street crammed with souvenir shops and ice cream parlours. On this occasion, there were only a handful of tourists huddled under dripping umbrellas. Everywhere smelt damp.

They entered a small café at the end of the main parade. It smelled of home cooking and pine fires. The ceiling beams were cut into the rock and two customers sitting on one of the tables at the back were eating inside the cave itself. The only other patrons were two older Frenchmen standing up at the bar with tiny *espresso* coffee cups in front of them. Jean-Marc seemed to know the waiter, who greeted him warmly.

"May I introduce you to Monsieur Michel Roches, a cousin of my mother's."

Monsieur Roches had a shaggy dark moustache. He wore a black waistcoat and trousers and a white, pocketed apron tied around his waist. The sleeves of his white shirt were rolled up to just below his elbows. He chatted to the children in French, with Alice and Jean-Marc translating if Robert didn't understand.

"What! You have ridden here on a scooter... and so close to the river! There have been severe weather warnings on the radio today, my young friends," he warned. "If this rain doesn't stop soon, the river will burst its banks. Many towns and villages in this part of the Dordogne will be flooded."

Alice remembered the scenes of devastation they had seen in the swirling visions of Eidor the Shaman.

"What do you want to eat then?" asked Monsieur Roches, showing them to a cozy table close to the crackling fire and passing them each a menu.

They all ordered the chocolate cake that Jean-Marc recommended and hot chocolate to drink. Jean-Marc passed Alice her half of the stone and put his half on the table in front of him. They were silent.

"It seems to me," began Jean-Marc eventually, "that if we have to go back, then we'll have to try and time it for a few minutes after we left there, to avoid those two princes again."

"I think it might be a good idea if we took a torch," said Robert. "It was really dark in that inner cave... I will have the sword though!"

"Oh. Come on, Rob!" said Alice. "You're no match for Prince Richard. He'd have killed you if it hadn't been for Kuy!"

Robert shrugged his shoulders.

"Do you think we could try and go straight into that cave then, the one with the skeleton?" said Jean-Marc.

There was a pause. No one looked all that keen to rush back to a dark burial chamber complete with skeleton.

At that moment, their food arrived and they tucked into their snack hungrily.

Alice was the first to finish. She sat in silence, sipping her hot chocolate and fiddling with her stone. She was deep in thought. If they were going to return, it would be easiest if they tried now, before her aunt came back, otherwise it might prove difficult to get to the cave again.

She was rubbing her stone in the way she had grown accustomed to before she had known of its magic or her own powers. She started to feel a bit sick. At first, she thought all that chocolate might have been a mistake. Then she realised. She was going to have another vision or dream or whatever it was that she could do.

The power cursed through her veins and once more, she found herself watching a scene from the past.

This time, she was in the darkened, smoky, fire-lit bedroom of the dwelling that had once stood on the site of the eagle sanctuary.

"Kuy!" she muttered.

She recognised the cloaked figure of the seer. He was accompanied by the Lady Clare, and by the armoured squire. They were sweaty and breathless.

Alice strained to understand what they were saying.

"Please! There must be something you can do!" said Lady Clare.

"I do not have the power, my Lady. Has John told you of the curse?"

"In part. He said it had something to do with the broken pendant."

"Indeed it does. John was warned, along with his brother, of the possible consequences of taking the stone."

"His brother? You mean ..."

"Yes. The King. They were together when it was taken."

"Is King Richard cursed too?"

"Yes."

The seer paused as if in a dream.

"It is now his destiny to die young. His greed will destroy him soon."

The squire took a small breath in surprise, but Lady Clare did not look concerned.

"And John? He will be king if Richard dies."

"He will not live happily either, I fear. I have seen visions of much misery and fighting around him and I have sensed treachery, poison and painful death."

Lady Clare looked down at Alys of France.

"But Alys... she cannot recover from these terrible injuries. She is close to death. Why must she suffer too?"

The seer was silent. He seemed unsure.

Alice found the smoke unbearable and she coughed to clear her throat.

The seer turned instantly.

Alice drew her breath. She had thought she was invisible but the seer took a step towards her. He closed his eyes and raised his arms slightly, inhaling deeply.

"What is it?" said the squire in alarm. He and Lady Clare were looking in Alice's direction.

"There's no-one there, is there?" asked Lady Clare.

A smile crept across the seer's face. He opened his eyes. For one moment, he looked directly into Alice's eyes and she felt a wave of warmth pass through her body. Kuy the Seer turned back towards the bed.

"There is nothing to fear for Alys, my friends. I do not see her death. In fact, I see happiness after all her suffering, but not with Richard or John. When Richard returns soon, he will release her from her vows and she will be free." He paused and shuddered. His eyes glazed in a sorrowful, far away look. "But those two, your king and your prince, they will not escape the curse though,

110

as I once warned them. Neither will live long and they will both die violent deaths, Richard in a castle not far from here and John in a castle in England."

Lady Clare raised her eyebrows in disbelief.

The seer closed his eyes, raised his hands over the still body of Alys of France and began chanting a low, melodious song in an ancient language. He turned his palms upward and slowly drew them towards the low, beamed ceiling.

As he did so, Alys of France opened her eyes and blinked.

Outside, a bell tolled in one of the chapels of Rocamadour.

"It is a miracle!" gasped Lady Clare, and she knelt down at the bedside and started to weep.

Kuy the Seer turned, wrapped his cloak around him and walked towards the door. He paused close to Alice and stared intently.

21

Plastic Capes and Flaming Trees

Kuy's penetrating gaze transfixed Alice.

"Fulfill your destiny and she will be saved," he murmured, his arm gesturing behind him towards the bed.

Then he stepped back and vanished through the doorway.

Alice flopped forward onto the table, just missing her empty plate and opened her eyes to find Robert shaking her.

"Alice! Alice!"

She sat up and rubbed her head.

"Did you fall asleep? You were muttering."

"No," said Jean-Marc. "You've had another vision, haven't you?"

"Yes," whispered Alice.

Even though she felt exhausted, she knew what they must do.

"We must go back."

Jean-Marc looked dubiously at the heavy rain outside.

"Well, if we're going, it had better be now. Remember what Monsieur Roches said about the river. It could flood any time."

The three adventurers looked at each other grimly before pushing back their chairs. Monsieur Roches frowned.

"Surely you're not going back out in that? Can't I ring someone for you? It's really dangerous out there. You can stay here... I could use some help in the kitchen you know!"

Although he was joking, he looked very worried.

"We'll be O.K. Honestly. But thanks for the concern," said Jean-Marc.

"And thanks for the hot chocolate, Monsieur," said Alice.

"Then at least you could use these..."

The jovial Frenchman took three clear plastic rain capes from a basket of souvenirs in front of the counter. The capes were covered in printed silhouettes of Rocamadour with the town's name underneath. The printing came in a variety of bright colours. The children eyed the hideous objects suspiciously.

"Please. I insist! I know they are not the height of fashion, but they will keep you dry at least, and... they are free!"

The children looked at each other and burst out laughing. Jean-Marc reached out and took the generous gifts. He passed them around.

"Come on, guys!" he joked. "We're going to look really something on the moped in these!"

"I'm just glad none of the class can see me like this!" said Robert, pulling the hood up over his head and doing a twirl for the others.

"Cool, actually," said Alice.

"Yeah! Yeah! I bet!"

"Come on, let's get going," said Jean-Marc. "Thanks, Michel! See you around!"

They started down the street towards the moped.

"Oh, no! A torch!" said Robert suddenly.

"I'll go back!" said Jean-Marc. "I bet Michel will have one!"

He tossed the keys at Robert and ran back into the café. As soon as the other two reached the bike, Robert fiddled with the key until the padlock sprang open. He was just reversing when Jean-Marc returned brandishing a large black torch triumphantly.

"Well done!" said Alice.

"Good old Michel!" panted Jean-Marc. He threw the torch at Alice to hold. She caught it deftly. "Come on!"

Jean-Marc took the handlebars from Robert with a nod of appreciation and they climbed back on. Robert's see-through cape flapped furiously behind as the scooter sped once more towards the troglodyte city.

Somewhere up above, through the driving rain, Alice thought she heard the piercing cry of large bird of prey. She glanced at the river. The rushing waters lashed the top of its grassy banks, and in some places lapping waves ebbed and swirled over the top. She thought of home, and wondered how far the River Trent had risen. If Aunt Bonnie was right, the centre of Newark might well be flooded by now.

Suddenly, Jean-Marc slowed right down and Alice and Robert peered over his shoulder. The river had finally burst here and water flowed right across the road. A car coming the other way drove slowly through, sending up sparkling flumes on both sides.

"We can make it," said Robert.

"Lift your legs then!" said Jean-Marc. He revved the engine, and the little motorbike lurched forward into the water.

"Wick ... ed!" yelled Robert.

"Better than a roller-coaster!" screamed Alice, gripping Jean-Marc tightly.

The sturdy moped wheels generated dazzling arcs of splashing water around them. They all shrieked with laughter as they shot back onto dry road the other side.

"Aunt Bonnie would die if she knew what we were doing!" said Alice.

"Hang on. We're almost there!" yelled Jean-Marc over his shoulder.

They strained to see ahead through the curtain of rain. A moment later, the hulk of ancient cavernous rock that concealed so many secrets loomed sinisterly through the mists.

They propped the bike against some railings in the empty car park.

"Something's wrong," said Jean-Marc as they walked towards the gates. "The place is deserted."

Even in the gift shop was locked when Robert tried the door. Jean-Marc ran up to the turnstile and found a thick chain round it.

"Now what are we going to do?"

Alice was surveying the height of the turnstile.

"We climb over it," she said.

"That's breaking and entering... we might get caught," said Robert.

"Do you see anyone else?" said Alice.

Robert and Jean-Marc looked gingerly around them. "Well... no... but..."

"Exactly. Come on! We have to go up there!"

Alice found a groove for one of her feet about a metre up and levered herself onto the barrier. She crouched momentarily on the top before jumping off and landing deftly on the other side. Robert copied her. After a last furtive glance behind him, Jean-Marc followed. They started up the path towards the caves above.

Rushing water was cascading down the once dusty track, converting it into a mountain stream. Alice stumbled several times, and Robert's cape ripped against the rocky wall. The torrential rain whipped against their faces.

Without warning, a monstrous clap boomed out of the mists above. The three children froze while the thunder echoed in and out of the hollow caves around them.

"It seems a long way up here!" shouted Robert, wiping water from his face and spitting it from his mouth. "Have we missed the entrance to the cave?"

"I don't think so," yelled Jean-Marc. "It's round the next bend."

Suddenly, not far in front of them, a fork of lightning sizzled down to earth, striking a nearby tree with a deafening crack. It exploded into golden red flames. Almost in slow motion, the flaming tree started to fall towards them.

"In here!" screamed Robert as he lunged under an over hanging rock. Just in time, the other two leapt towards him, as the burning foliage rolled past. It bounced past their ledge and continued down the side of the hill. The flames hissed and went out as it tumbled through the wet undergrowth. Its descent was finally halted by a clump of trees on the riverbank.

Alice's heart was beating as fast and as hard as it had ever done. The three of them were silent for several minutes. It was Jean-Marc who spoke first.

"Well... shall we go on?"

"I... yes... come on! We've got this far!" said Robert valiantly.

Alice looked at him and then at Jean-Marc.

"We must be mad!" she muttered and she stepped back out into the rain.

22

A Last Journey

They battled on with their heads bowed against the violence of the storm.

"It's as if..." said Alice, gasping and panting. "...as if there's some kind of evil trying to stop us!"

At last they made it to the shelter of the cave and flopped against the craggy walls to get their breath back.

Robert wrenched off his torn cape and walked over to the back of the cave to examine the pile of rocks in the corner.

"I think... yes, if we stand about here... and think of arriving there as soon as Richard and John have gone... that should do it!"

Alice levered herself up and pulled off her cape. She felt in her pocket and extracted her half of the stone.

"Are we ready then?" said Jean-Marc.

The others nodded.

"Have the torch ready, Alice. I've got the sword," said Robert, linking arms with her.

"We're just going to go in, put back the stone and get out... yes?" said Jean-Marc.

Robert suddenly let go of Alice.

"Hang on! How are we going to get back if we leave the stones there?"

The other two looked at each other in dismay. Nobody had thought of that.

Alice gazed out into the rain. Once again, she thought she heard the cry of an eagle. She looked down at the stone in the palm of her hand.

"There must be a way," she said eventually. "Eidor

would not have meant for us to stay back in time, I'm sure of it."

"How sure?" said Robert.

"Very sure!"

Jean-Marc looked into the sparkling blue of Alice's eyes.

"I think she's right. Let's do it!" He held out his hand for her half of the stone.

Alice gave it to him and gripped his other hand. Reluctantly, Robert took Alice's arm.

"Concentrate on where we want to be!" said Jean-Marc. He closed his eyes.

Once again, they were all spinning in a rainbow of sensations, journeying through time itself.

With a bump, they landed. This time, they didn't hesitate. Robert sprang up, brandishing his weapon menacingly and they looked around. Thankfully, there was no sign of the Plantagenet princes.

"Sshhh! What's that?" whispered Robert.

There was a faint sound coming from the low corridor that lead from the outer cave into the painted burial chamber.

"Oh, no! Don't say they've gone back in there!" whispered Jean-Marc desperately. "We'll have no chance!"

"Sshhh!" Alice crept towards the opening and listened. "I think it's chanting . . . yes! It's O.K. It's the seer."

The other two strained to hear, but before they could say or do anything, Alice switched on the torch and started down the corridor.

"Alice!" they called together.

But it was too late. She was out of sight. The two boys ran after her, one behind the other, stooping to avoid the jagged ceiling.

Around the bend, they saw her. The chanting had stopped and Alice stood face to face with the seer, silhouetted against the crimson glow of the fire.

Kuy, the medieval Minstrel of Aquitaine, had painted his face with red markings very similar to those that Alice and Jean-Marc had seen on Eidor. His chest was bare now and they could see that he too wore three copper rings above one elbow and the other arm was tattooed with the same red and black triangular marks.

"I have been waiting," he said. "For a moment, I thought the spirits were deceiving me, or that evil spirits might be working to prevent your coming. But I see that all is well. Come in, please."

Robert was still looking furtively behind them, for signs of pursuit. "Where are..."

"They have gone. They will not come back. At least not yet. John's squire will return one day with the Lady Clare, and ask for my help to save Lady Alys. But you know all that." They nodded.

"You know why we are here, don't you?" she said.

"Of course." He beckoned to them to come further into the cave, closer to the remains of the Stone Age queen.

"But how will we get back?" asked Jean-Marc, voicing all their thoughts.

Kuy the Seer chuckled.

"Then you do not wish to remain in this age of violence and war?"

They shook their heads.

"A pity! We could have achieved so much!"

The seer scooped some powder from a platter beside him and threw it onto the fire. The flames sparked and crackled and a purple smoke filled the room with a deep, sensuous aroma.

"Is it possible to stay?" said Alice.

The boys looked at her in horror.

"Yes. Of course. You have the power to choose your destiny. But you can only stay behind once. If you remain now, then you will never travel the highways of time again."

"Again?" said Robert.

"Yes. You are time travellers, like me and many others in this universe. You will travel many times, if it is your destiny. From now on you will recognise Time Triggers if they cross your path. It will be up to you to decide on how to use them."

"But I didn't find one of the stones this time," said Robert, a little sheepishly.

"No. And without one, you were lost at the beginning. For a time, your will was at the mercy of evil spirits who tried to use you to corrupt the path of destiny. I am right, am I not?"

"Well... yes... I did do some odd things."

"That explains it!" said Alice, grinning at Robert.

"Will I find a Time Trigger of my own one day?"

"I think it is likely, young man, now that your power has been exposed. But that will be for the spirits to decide."

"Kuy, you said that there are many time travellers in the universe. Can we recognise each other in any way?" asked Alice.

"Only if it is your destiny to know one another."

The pungent aromas in the painted cave were making Alice dizzy. The bison and reindeer danced on the walls around her. She knelt down, close to the skull of the long-dead queen.

"We must do what we came to do," she said, looking at Jean-Marc, who was still holding the stones.

"But how do we get back?" he said.

"It is easy, my friends. You must chose something of this time that you would like to keep and touch it against the Time Trigger. It will soak up just enough of the Trigger's energy to take you back. But after that, it will simply be a souvenir!"

"Wow!" said Robert, looking fondly at his sword.

"Anything?" said Jean-Marc.

The seer nodded.

"Can I have this?" Jean-Marc pointed to a bear claw that rested alongside the body of the queen. "It would look wonderful in my collection." The seer nodded with a smile.

"And what will you choose?" he asked Alice.

Alice looked around her.

"I wish I could take the paintings!" she sighed wistfully.

The seer held up the beautiful shell necklace that Alice had once seen around the queen's neck. "What about this?"

"Oh! I couldn't! It belongs to her."

"On the contrary, my young Lady. It was the custom to leave objects with the dead that might help those of other times and other worlds. By returning the stone to its rightful resting-place, you have helped so many. The spirits can rest now." He smiled mischievously. "I have been keeping it for you. Do you not recall that it was missing when John and Richard came upon this place?"

Alice nodded her head in silence. Kuy held it out for her.

"Take it, Alice!" said Robert.

Alice accepted the treasure and held it lovingly in her hands.

"Now, my friends, you must touch your tokens on the Time Trigger and then place it back inside the amulet."

Jean-Marc lay the broken pieces of the stone side by side on the ground in front of them. Then he held his bear claw against them.

"Oh! It tingles... and it's so warm... all up my arm!"

Then Robert knelt down on one knee and touched the jewelled grip of his medieval sword against the fragments of meteorite.

"Wow!" he said softly. "I can feel it too... like warm energy passing into my body!"

At last it was Alice's turn. She hesitated. There was something powerful and sensuous about this cave with its delicate paintings and pungent scent, and about Kuy the medieval seer. She felt drained and tired.

"You must go now, my child, if you wish to return to your own time," he said. "Your work is done... for now."

Alice felt a fresh surge of hope and excitement. She knelt beside the skeleton of the long dead queen, and gently brushed the shell necklace across the two halves of their stone. Immediately, she felt the wave of tingling power rushing through her fingers and into her body.

"Now, replace the stone," said Kuy.

With trembling fingers, Alice picked up the two pieces. To her surprise, the stones felt warm for the first time, almost burning her hand. She gently opened the laced neck of the leather amulet. A silent tear trickled down her dirty cheek.

"Good-bye, my friends," said Kuy.

Robert and Jean-Marc watched as Alice slid the two stone pieces into the pouch. There was an instant, blinding flash of purest white and the children fell back, covering their eyes.

23

The Festival of Montignac

Someone was shouting at them.

"Alice! Alice! What do you think you're doing?"

Aunt Bonnie was walking briskly up the track towards them. She was clearly annoyed.

Alice rubbed her eyes and shook her head. She felt so giddy that she didn't dare to stand up. She looked around at the boys. They were obviously in the same state. In fact, they looked rather comical, and Alice started to laugh.

"Young lady, I don't find this funny at all! I nearly did myself an injury climbing over that turnstile," said her aunt crossly. "Whatever have you been doing, you're filthy dirty... and who are these two?"

Alice stopped laughing and tried to look remorseful. But somehow the picture of her aunt clambering over the iron turnstile made her giggle again, despite her best efforts not to.

Aunt Bonnie looked at the three of them in desperation. Much to Alice's relief, her aunt sat down on the large boulder behind her and folded her arms with a not-so-fierce frown on her face, waiting for an explanation.

"You haven't been drinking wine have you?" she suddenly asked, suspiciously.

Alice felt her strength returning and sat up.

"No, Bonnie. Don't worry! We've just been messing about in these caves, that's all."

"These caves are closed!"

"Yes, I know... I just needed to... well, we..."

"Oh, spare me the details!"

Aunt Bonnie jumped up.

"Come on! Let's get out of here before the staff come back and call the *gendarmes*."

She strode off back down towards the exit.

"She's all right, your aunt," said Robert. He stood up and brushed centuries old dirt from his jeans.

"Oh!" he exclaimed, looking down at his sword. It was rusty and blunt and very old looking now. He blew the debris from the grip, and smiled as he saw the gleam of the jewels beneath. "This is gonna need some polish!"

Jean-Marc was examining his bear claw. Happily it seemed intact. Alice's necklace was dusty but undamaged too.

"How are we going to explain all these?" said Jean-Marc.

"We got them in a souvenir shop," said Robert in a very matter-of-fact sort of voice. "They're worthless souvenirs." He shrugged his shoulders.

"I suppose we did, really, didn't we?" said Alice, slightly absent-mindedly, admiring her very own archeological treasure.

Then she remembered her aunt.

"Come on!" she shouted, running off down the track. "We'd better not make Bonnie any more cross."

Aunt Bonnie was leaning on her rusty old Renault, waiting for them in the car park. Thankfully, there was still no one else about.

Suddenly, Alice realised something.

"It's stopped raining!"

"Ha! Cool or what!" said Robert nodding and looking around in amazement.

Jean-Marc grinned and offered the other two the thumbs up sign.

In fact, the sun was shining brightly and the sky had turned back to a deep turquoise colour. One or two last clouds were drifting away over the horizon and the children felt the welcome warmth drying their wet clothes. Even the river was calm now, although still very full in places.

"We must have left those gorgeous capes up there!" laughed Alice.

"Thank goodness!" said Robert.

"Do you think you might introduce me to your two handsome friends then, Alice?" said her aunt. She wasn't angry any more.

"Oh, sorry! This is Robert. He's from my school. And this is Jean-Marc... er, he lives on the farm we're staying on."

"I see. Pleased to meet you both."

Aunt Bonnie shook hands with the boys.

"Well. I don't know what you've been up to... oh, don't look so worried, Alice! I don't want to know either. The important thing is that you're safe."

Alice breathed a sigh of relief.

"How did you two get here?" asked Aunt Bonnie.

Jean-Marc pointed to his muddy moped.

Bonnie raised her eyebrows and was about to ask something, but then decided not to.

"Really? Well, fine... whatever! Are you going back the same way, or do you want a lift?"

"Um, thanks everso," said Robert. "But I think we'd better go back the same way we came... I'm not really supposed to be here..."

"Don't tell me!"

On the way back, Alice and her aunt listened to the car radio. Alice lay back and watched the scenery passing by. The regimental rows of neatly trimmed vines were once again drenched in sunshine. In fact, the vineyards and walnut groves and tobacco plants were steaming as the rain evaporated under the kiss of the hot sun. Café owners were putting out their tables again and hanging out baskets of flowers. Shutters were flung back and doors opened.

"Has it stopped raining in England too?" asked Alice suddenly.

"Oh, I don't know. I hope so." Bonnie fiddled with the radio and eventually found a channel that was broadcasting the news. It wasn't very good reception, but in between the crackles, Alice could just make out what was being said. There was a lot about the flooding in this part of France and how the rain had suddenly stopped, just in time to avoid catastrophe. Alice smiled with satisfaction as she thought about her enormous and powerful secret.

At the very end of the bulletin came the news Alice had been hoping for. The flash flooding in the English Midlands was also receding. Despite official predictions, the heavy rain had apparently stopped suddenly at about the same time as in southern France.

"Your mum and dad must be relieved," said Aunt Bonnie.

"Yep!" said Alice. She felt for the necklace in her pocket. As her fingers caressed the fascinating shapes of the shells, she remembered Kuy the Seer, and Richard, John and Alys of France.

The sun was close to setting as they drove into the town. A few early grasshoppers were already warming up for the night. Alice wondered where they had been hiding during the rain.

"Oh, yes! I almost forgot," said Aunt Bonnie. "Your teacher, Miss Wotnot, rang. The disco's cancelled... floodwater in the D.J's garage or something. Anyway, I've arranged to get you all in at the Festival of Montignac tonight instead."

Alice grinned in delight.

And it was an evening to remember. After sunset, the townsfolk lit hundreds of candles and switched on a myriad of coloured fairy lights on either side of the bridge that spanned the river. This year there was more than usual to celebrate since the rain had stopped.

Locals and tourists poured in to join in the festivities. Dancers from all over the world were in town tonight, dressed in a spectacular array of beautiful costumes. The pulsing music was loud and exciting.

"I hope this young lady was on her best behaviour," said Miss Walton to Aunt Bonnie, as she arrived with Mr Hutchinson at the head of the chattering English children.

"Absolutely!" replied Bonnie before giving her worried niece a mischievous wink.

Alice looked around for Robert. Suddenly, he pounced with his hands over her eyes.

"Urhh... ummm... I wonder? Let me guess... Could it be ... Prince John or even King Richard?"

Robert let go and gave her an affectionate punch on one arm.

"I think that I can safely say that I'm a better catch than either of them," he said.

Before long Alice was sharing a meal with her friends and family, joking and listening to the exotic music under a canopy of stars.

Suddenly, with a surge of bravery, Robert pushed back his chair and walked round the table to Alice. He held out his hand.

"Would you like to dance?"

He was confident and determined and his blue eyes shone beneath his mop of thick, blond hair. Alice was impressed. In silence she stood up and took his hand. Right in front of their gawping classmates, he lead her into the centre of the square, now swirling with dancers, and they disappeared from view.

Alice and Robert danced until they were both too

hot and thirsty to continue.

"Can anyone join in the fun?" called a boy's voice with a thick French accent.

"Hey!" cheered Robert as Jean-Marc approached.

"Your ears must be burning. We were just wondering if you'd make it!" said Alice.

"How could I miss this! Have you danced yet?"

"We have!" said Robert.

"Ah . . . but have you *really* danced?"

Alice and Robert looked at him blankly.

"Then allow me!"

Jean-Marc took Alice by the arm, almost lifting her from her chair, and swept her onto the dance floor, twirling and embracing her in perfect time to the music. After several dances, they flopped down exhausted. Robert grinned and nodded in admiration, raising his glass.

In hushed voices, they spoke on of ancient curses and medieval princes and wondered among themselves whether any of them would find a Time Trigger to give them the power to travel again.